MW00487409

THE COWBOY'S RUNAWAY BRIDE

THE WYOMING MATCHMAKER SERIES

KRISTI ROSE

Vintage Housewife Books

The
COWBOY'S
Run Away
BRIDE

USA Today Bestselling Author
KRISTI ROSE

Copyright © 2018 by **Kristi Rose**

All rights reserved. No part of this publication may be reproduced, distributed or transmitted in any form or by any means, without prior written permission.

Vintage Housewife Books

PO BOX 842

Ridgefield, WA 98642

www.kristirose.net

Publisher's Note: This is a work of fiction. Names, characters, places, and incidents are a product of the author's imagination. Locales and public names are sometimes used for atmospheric purposes. Any resemblance to actual people, living or dead, or to businesses, companies, events, institutions, or locales is completely coincidental.

Book Layout © 2018 Vellum

Cover Design © 2018 The Killion Group

Editing by CMD Writing and Editing

THE COWBOY'S RUNAWAY BRIDE/ Kristi Rose. -- _1st ed._

ISBN- Print 978-1-944513-28-3

ISBN-eBooks 978-1-944513-27-6

JOIN MY NEWSLETTER

AND GET A FREE BOOK

Hi

If you'd like to be the first to know about my sales and new releases then join my newsletter. As part of my reader community you will have access to giveaways, freebies, bonus content and receive a free book.

Sound like you might be interested? Give me a try. You can always unsubscribe at any time.

www.kristirose.net

XOXO,

TUESDAY

I f it weren't for bad luck, Ellie Green wouldn't have any luck at all.

She stared down at the back passenger tire of her truck. The tire was so flat the rubber spilled out onto the pavement like it had been poured there. Her truck was actually listing to one side. She wondered what she'd done to tick off the universe. Whatever it was must have been something *big* because the bad luck hits just kept coming. Today alone, she had burned the front tail of her favorite light-yellow flannel shirt on the stove, but thankfully only the corner was singed away. Though she'd half expected it to go up in flames and used the first thing she'd had on hand to extinguish it. Which was cranberry juice.

To make matters worse, she was getting a zit on her chin, and it felt like a big one. Possibly the size of her nose. These events were the sum of her day, and it wasn't even noon. She'd experienced this sort of nonsense for a while now and was getting tired of it.

Ellie rested her forearm along the side of the truck's bed and her forehead on her arm. She stared at the flat through the gap between her arm and her body. She needed a plan, but her tired brain struggled to come up with one. Behind her, the sound of scuffling cowboy boots drew near. She hadn't expected black Tony Lama shit-kickers to come into her view next to the tire. She'd figured whoever it was would keep on walking to the diner.

"You trying to will it to inflate?" said the man belonging to the boots.

Ellie straightened on a sigh, then turned to the person asking the question. She didn't recognize him, but he looked like every other cowboy around here, restless and looking for the next thrill. Because she didn't know him, she figured she really didn't have to be nice. Right now, polite required too much energy.

So she said, "I tried blowing it like a balloon, but nothing." Seriously, did he really think she was just standing here willing her tire to inflate? Okay, she *had* done that the instant she'd seen the tire, but wishes only came true in the movies, and she'd quickly set those hopes aside.

"I reckon you'll have to go to plan B," he said without so much as a smile or hint of teasing. He casually leaned against the truck.

Ellie studied him, trying to figure out if he was someone whose acquaintance had slipped her mind. He was acting awfully familiar with her, like they'd met before. He dressed like a cowboy from around these parts. Not that his clothes meant anything, but Wolf Creek, Wyoming was a small town. Everyone knew each other. There were no six degrees of separation here. But this guy... Though there was something about him that felt familiar, she didn't know his face. At. All.

Everything about his look was dark, including his scowl. She scanned him from the top down. His hair was midnight black and cut in what she knew the military called a high and tight. Rich, dark brown eyes inspected her, too and she struggled to look away. He was dressed in a black T-shirt worn under a black and dark green flannel shirt with the sleeves rolled up to his elbows. His muscular arms looked chiseled from granite. His dark indigo-washed jeans fit snugly over powerful thighs. He was lethal to girls who liked that sort of look. She wasn't so frivolous.

"How exactly would you define plan B?" She wasn't worried for her safety. She was outside the diner and the good folks of Wolf Creek were inside eating the meals she'd cooked. Her shift, as the morning short order cook, ended not more than ten minutes ago. And those good folks liked her cooking almost as much as they liked their gossip. They wouldn't let something happen to her. Who would make them breakfast tomorrow? Who else knew the elder Mr. Landry liked parsley on his eggs? Ellie did.

"Plan B would be to put the spare on," he said matter of fact.

She expected him to follow up his statement with a "duh."

"Gee, what a good idea. Wish I had thought of that." She skirted around him to the other side of the truck and pointed to the passenger tire on the driver's side. "Only 'my spare' is right here. See, I had a flat yesterday and did exactly that. Put the spare on." She wagged her fingers at him. "I even used my own two little hands. Today, the situation is different, wouldn't you say?" She was being intentionally snarky and planted her hands on her hips. This poor, dark stranger was going to feel the force of her irritation, and there was nothing she could do to stop it. Her anger, frustration, and fear had been mounting for days.

Ellie almost snorted with a laugh at her jaded thoughts. Seemed like the universe didn't like him too much either if it sent him into her path.

When Dark Stranger strode around to her, his left leg dragged some and made the shuffling sound she'd heard earlier. He had a limp, but it was so subtle she almost missed it. Had she not heard it, she probably would have never seen it.

He stopped short when he saw her spare, of the donut variety, already on her truck. He considered her, his expression puzzled.

She said, "Its on my list today to swing by the gas station and pick up my new tire."

He pointed to the donut. "You got this flat yesterday?" He waited for her answer, a nod, then moved to the front tire where he squatted down and began to run his hands over the tread. He did this to each of her tires, including what he could of the flat one.

She followed him as he worked his way around her truck. "Yeah, I checked all the tires for nails or screws or something." She shook her head. "Nothing's there."

"You drive through any broken glass or construction sites?" He was still squatting by the tires and shifted his weight. A slight grimace etched his face as he did so. It was gone as quickly as it had shown up.

"Nope. Not that I noticed, and considering I had a flat yesterday, I was extra attentive today when I drove to work. Nothing." She drove the same route every single day. From Grams's house, where she currently lived, to the diner for work, to Williamses' ranch to feed their livestock while they were out of town, and then back home to do chores and man the farm stand. On Tuesdays and Wednesdays, she added in the delivery of her goat milk soaps and lotions to stores on main street, stopped by the feed store, occasionally the vet's office after going to the Williamses', all before heading home. Regardless of the day, she did a complete circle comprising of home, town, and the Williamses' ranch.

Dark Stranger ran his hands over the tire again before reaching up to the bed and pulling himself to a stand. "Let's get this tire off, and I'll take you down to Carl's garage." He side shuffled to the back of the truck, then reached across the bed to fidget with a latch of the diamond tread toolbox. The top popped open. She was surprised the lid opened so easily considering how dented the top was.

He ran his hand over the dents. Most were the same size and shape as if done by the same object. "This top looks like it's taken a beating."

Ellie shrugged. "It's been that way forever." Of course, she wasn't going to share with Dark Stranger that her frustrations and a tire iron had added all the dents to the toolbox last week. Not that she cared what he thought. The information wasn't any of his business.

"Forever you say?" He arched his brows when he glanced at her. "You should write the company and tell them how impressive their aluminum is, not a rust spot in the dents whatsoever."

Not knowing what else to say, she shrugged again.

His lips twitched as he considered her. His gaze flicked down to her chin where she could feel the zit growing larger every nanosecond.

"I can do that," she said and stepped toward him, holding her hand out for the iron.

"I don't mind helping." He pulled out a tire jack and shoved it under the truck.

Ellie went to stand in front of the flat tire. "I appreciate it, but I'm just gonna call Carl at the garage and have him come and get me. I'll take care of this." She took the tire iron from his hand.

"I don't mind helping," he repeated. Probably because he thought she needed to be reminded.

She said with more ire than intended, "I don't need help."

Dark stranger stared at her, his brow slightly furrowed as if he wasn't sure she meant what she said.

So she added. "You were going into the diner to eat, right?"

He nodded. "Yeah."

"Then you better get going before all the moms with their toddlers arrive. They always take the best pastries."

For what felt like minutes, but was likely seconds, they stood there and considered each other. Ellie had her back against her truck, wishing he'd move on already. She didn't have time for any more trouble or nonsense.

Dark stranger broke from the standoff first. "If you're sure?" His expression showed his skepticism.

She rolled her eyes. "Positive."

He shrugged as if to say "suit yourself" and shuffled off to the diner without so much as looking back, his left leg dragging ever so slightly.

Having a stranger offer their help wasn't unappreciated. Ellie just preferred not to be indebted to anyone. Nothing good came from it anyway.

2

TUESDAY

Truth was, Shane Hannigan could have happily walked by the woman with the mile-long legs, the mop of blond, crazy curly hair and flat tire without so much as a second glance. His mood was *that* foul and getting fouler by the minute. The running tab on his bad state of mind was well into three weeks, two days and... heck, pretty much every single minute of every day. Beginning the moment after the doctor told him he was being discharged from rehab and his command suggested he take leave, go home, and wait out the results of the med board. Most active-duty Marines were allowed to continue with some portion of their work, even if limited in nature. He was of sound mind and, by his best guess, ninety-five percent of sound body, so there was no reason for him to not be on limited duty, or LIMDU as it was commonly referred. Apparently though, those who outranked him were making all the important decisions about his life.

The diner was quintessential with its Formica tabletops trimmed in aluminum and red vinyl chairs and bar stools. It's where gossip began and ended. Once inside, Shane lifted his guard higher. Here he might have to answer questions he wasn't ready to. Heaven forbid he had to repeat the story of his injury, one he couldn't remember. Concussions did that to people.

He slid onto a stool, the vinyl so worn it was cracked, and flipped his mug over indicating he wanted coffee. Sally, the diner's long-standing waitress, filled the mug without so much as a pleasant greeting. She'd attempted pleasantries the first few times he'd come since she'd graduated high school a few years before him and had tried going down memory lane, but she'd gotten nowhere. He was glad she'd given up.

He sensed someone come up behind him before he heard or saw anything. He took a deep breath, and the scent was all he needed. Vanilla and a sweet flowery aroma mixed with the subtle acrid smell of printing ink.

"What do you want, Cricket?" he asked his youngest sister. She must have been at work earlier this morning to already smell like ink. Cricket owned the one newspaper in town. She slid onto the stool beside him. Laura, the sister born between him and Cricket, had passed away a little over seven years ago in a motor vehicle accident. He tried not take his bad mood out on her and dug deep for patience. While he was fighting overseas, Cricket had been here at home, helping their parents pick up the pieces following Laura's unexpected death.

"Where were you last night?" Her voice was low, and there wasn't any accusation in her tone. He appreciated that about her.

She continued. "Not that I care who or what you were doing. Only that you're alive the next day to tell the tale."

He hated that she worried about him, but he hated being managed more. "Then why you wanna know where I was last night?" He focused on getting the coffee into his system, hoping the caffeine would reduce the headache he'd been battling.

"So we can have our stories straight when the parents question us later tonight at dinner." She faced him and rested her feet on the bar of his stool.

Like he'd done a million times since they were kids, he pushed them off with the tip of his boot. She instantly put her feet back on the bar. Shane pushed again. They would do this a few more times until one of them gave up. It used to be her but, lately, giving up had been all him. He blamed the lack of energy, the headaches, or whatever else he could come up with.

Sure enough, two rounds later he let her win.

"Why do we have to have a story for the parents?" Since returning to Wolf Creek, Shane had refused to stay at home. Instead, he hid out at Cricket's house in town. Being at home would have put him in the hands of his worried mother and observant father.

"Because Dad called last night and wanted you to come by."

He glanced at her. "Last night? He wanted me to come by then?"

She nodded. "Yeah. That's what he said. Said he tried you on your cell."

"I turned it off." And after he'd taken care of some business, he'd sat for hours in his truck, parked off the side of some road between here and Cody, staring out at the open prairies before him. He used to love looking at the land, never once felt as if the mountains were cutting him off from the world, never saw them as a barrier. Until now.

As a kid, he used to run wild across the land, reveling in the freedom it allowed, knowing he could follow a main road and it would take him to the other side of the country. Now the mountains boxed him in, acting as prison guards, challenging him to try to cross over, promising a hardship if he dared. Taunting him, telling him he was not allowed over. No one on the other side wanted him.

Last night, or the wee hours of this morning to be precise, he'd pulled off the road and sat in the middle of some random prairie and thrown one hell of a pity party. Shane ran a hand down his two-day-old beard. This was not how he saw his life turning out.

Cricket put her hand on his forearm. "You should call Dad. Tell him whatever you want. If you need me to corroborate it, give me a heads up." She squeezed and let go. "All I said was that you were out, and I'd pass the message along when I saw you."

"What do you think he wants?"

"He said he wanted your opinion about something and needed you to go by the feed store and get the supplies. But I think that was a front he was using."

He appreciated her honesty. He cast her a sideways glance. "Getting the supplies is Mark's job." Mark was the foreman on his family's ranch. Kyle, Javier, Moses, and Buck were the ranch hands. Every role was filled at the ranch. There, Shane was in the way. Anything he did would be taking away a job from one of the other guys, and Shane wasn't about to do that.

"What do you think he really wanted?" Shane could guess, but he wanted to see how accurate he was.

"He's checking up on you. Mom probably put him up to it. They don't like that you're staying with me because then they can't see for themselves how you're really doing. Throw them a bone. Go get the feed, let Mom make you lunch or something, complain that your leg hurts but you're doing whatever, don't mention medicine to deal with it, and then get out of there."

He groaned.

Cricket touched his arm again. "Shane, we lost Laura, and then we almost lost you. Please try and understand we need to see you and touch you to know you're still here. We're glad you came home intact."

He glanced at her hand on his arm then placed his over hers and squeezed. "Not all of me is intact. I left part of me on that street when that bomb went off."

She squeezed his hand back, then glanced at his leg before returning her attention to him. "Must have been the part of you where you housed your sense of humor, good mood, and shaving skills." She nodded slightly to his face and rolled her eyes.

Shane pushed her away. "Get out of my space. If I'm going to the ranch, I don't want to use up my tolerance for family with you."

Cricket snorted. "Too late." She stood.

Shane chuckled then snaked a hand out to grab her arm "Hey, what's up with the curly hair cutie outside?" He jerked his head in the direction of the windows. Cricket's gaze followed. He hated to ask. He told himself to mind his own business, to butt out. Yet, here he was, not butting out. He'd been raised to do the right thing, to protect the weak. It was one reason why he'd joined the Marines. Shane had no tolerance for others being targeted or mistreated. It went against his grain. Something told him the cutie with the meadow-green eyes a man could lose himself in and don't-help-me attitude was in a bad way. Two flat tires in the matter of a few days. He didn't like it. No, sir. So much so that he was considering getting further involved. As stupid as he thought the idea was.

"Ellie? Um, let's see. She moved here the year you went to college. Graduated with me. Don't you remember her?"

Shane shook his head.

"Lives with Minnie Greene. That's her granny."

"The veggie farm?" Minnie Greene was one of the nicest ladies he knew.

Cricket laughed. "Oh, you have no idea. Just wait."

"For what?"

"You'll see. But Ellie, she's the hardest working person I know. She has several jobs, and we can all set our watches by her." Cricket glanced at her wristwatch. "Right now, she's probably on her way to the Williams' ranch to feed their cattle."

Shane looked to the door then back at his sister. "She has a flat. You might not want to set your watch to her today. What's her deal?"

"Deal? She has no deal. She runs the farm with Minnie. I'm

guessing those two are keeping the place running with gum and duct tape. That's why she picked up all those other jobs."

"What happened to Earl?" he asked, referring to Minnie's husband.

"He passed a few year back. Paul, Ellie's Dad, came in long enough to help bury his dad and then split again to help those less fortunate than himself in some third-world country. You ask me, he should've stayed. He didn't have to go far to help someone because his mom was struggling, even then."

Shane shook his head. And here she wouldn't even let him help her change her tire.

"You remember crazy Mr. Phillips?"

Shane nodded. Phillips was the town's conspiracy theorist. If something went wrong in town, he pointed to aliens.

"He took a big hit when we had those fires last year. According to local gossip, he was playing fast and loose with insurance."

"Yeah? Like not having any?" Guessed Shane.

Cricket winked. "Exactly. Anyway, he's been helping out the Greenes as best he can from what I hear."

Shane sat back in disbelief. "That lunatic? Must be something in it for him." He glanced out the window. Carl had arrived and was loading the tire in the back of his truck. Shane returned his attention to Cricket, puzzled by what she was telling him.

Cricket shrugged. "Baffles me, too. But things around here have been weird since the fire. The Williams thought they were bankrupt, lost nearly everything in the fire. Some corporate energy guy came in, made them a sweet deal on some of their land, bought some rights or something. Now they travel half the year and stay here half the year. Keeping a small herd just because they can."

Cricket was right, becoming suddenly wealthy was unheard of around these parts. Even with the lottery.

He said, "Well, that's lucky." He realized if he'd spent more time with his sister and family, he might have already heard all this, but he'd been keeping people encounters to a minimum. The time had come for him to give the people who loved him what they needed. Time with him. He would start today.

"Wanna go to the ranch with me for lunch?" He caught Sally's eye and then pointed to the breakfast special on the menu. After she nodded, he returned the menu to its place against the napkin dispenser.

"Not on your life," she said, feigning mock horror, which dissolved into a laugh. She kept laughing as she walked away.

Shane chuckled. Laughter had been absent a long time in his life. His sour mood loosened its grip ever so slightly.

CRICKET SLID into the booth seat she'd vacated moments earlier to talk to Shane. She leaned forward and whispered to the women she'd been having breakfast with. "Remember how we were just discussing ideas to help Shane get back his smile?"

The three other women nodded. Cori, Cricket's closest friend, placed a hand on her massive baby bump. "Did you just ask him and he told you?"

Cricket shook her head. "He asked about Ellie."

Sabrina, who Cricket knew through Cori, held her index finger up. "Did he ask about Ellie and who she was dating?"

"No, he asked who she was."

"That doesn't mean anything, does it?" Hannah asked. A statics analyst by education, a wife and mother to twin boys by choice, she measured everything she could by a bell curve.

"I'm guessing it was *how* he asked about her," Sabrina said.

Cricket snapped her fingers then pointed to Sabrina. "Bingo. He called her a curly-haired cutie."

"Mm," the others said in unison.

"This gives us a good place to launch," Sabrina said.

Cori pointed to Sabrina. "This woman knows her stuff about getting couples together."

Cricket gathered up her purse. "I think I will be joining my brother at the folks for lunch after all, but first I've got to run by Minnie Greene's place while Ellie's out doing her other jobs."

Cricket slid from the booth following a chorus of well wishes from her friends. She made sure to slap her brother upside the head as she exited. Otherwise, he might get suspicious.

3

TUESDAY

Carl checked every single one of Ellie's tires for punctures again. He made sure each one was properly inflated, balanced, and told her to get on with her day, waving off her intentions to compensate him. "I can't take your money just cuz I put air in your tires. I got a machine around the side of the shop that'll do that for a few quarters."

"Exactly, so I should pay you." She waved her nearly maxed-out credit card toward him.

Carl shook his head. "Nope, that little blanket thingy you made for my granddaughter's car seat is a godsend. I should be paying you."

Carl, a red-headed man who was now almost all silver, was a handful of years away from obtaining his AARP senior citizen card. He'd become a first-time grandfather over Christmas. His oldest daughter, Mindy, had graduated college with a diploma and a positive pregnancy test. But whatever shock and parental disappointment Carl and his wife, Susan, might have experienced upon hearing Mindy's news was lost when they set eyes on their ginger-haired granddaughter, Ruby.

"She falls asleep in the car seat, and we just drop that cover you made over her and give her the rest she needs. Susan is particularly fond of the center slit you made so we can peak in on Ruby. And how smart were you to put snaps. When we'd gone baby-supply shopping with Mindy, we'd seen some with Velcro." Carl tapped the side of his head. "Whoever did that wasn't thinking." He made like he was pulling something apart "Rip! And the baby is awake. Dumbest idea. Ever."

Ellie laughed. "I guess that person never had a baby."

"Or they had one that never slept, and it's their prank on the rest of the world. But do you see why I can't charge you? Between that cover and the christening gown and quilt—"

"I love to sew, Carl, and sewing for a baby is exceptionally fun. Besides, I can only make so many sweaters and pajamas for the goats." Ellie was the proud momma to five special needs goats. Each goat, with the exception of her first goat, Benny the Jet, had been re-homed to her farm by the local veterinarian. The goats had been abandoned or dropped off like unwanted garbage outside the vet's office. Bryce, the vet, knew Ellie had Benny the Jet thriving. Bryce asked Ellie if she was willing to take in another. And then another. And another. And so on.

Carl handed over her keys. "When Ruby gets a little older, I want to bring her out to see the goats, if that's okay?"

"It sure is. Cori Besingame has taken pictures of children with the goats, and they've turned out adorable. Something to think about."

"I will." His smile was quickly erased from his face. "Now, listen. I can't explain what's going on with your tires except to say someone is purposefully letting the air out. I don't like it. Stuff like that doesn't happen in our town."

Except it was.

Ellie sucked in a slow breath. She didn't want Carl to see how rattled she really was. "Maybe it's a harmless prank. Not one I'm particularly enjoying, but every time I've gotten the flat, I've been somewhere safe." She tossed up her hands as if to say "who knew?" "I can't figure it out, to be honest."

Carl pointed a fatherly finger at her. "Well, you just keep me on speed dial, and I'll come get you, day or night. Got it?"

Ellie smiled. "Got it. Thanks, Carl."

He glanced at his watch. "Now get out of here. You're about twenty minutes behind schedule," he teased.

Ellie jumped. "The heck you say. Not rain, snow, or heat can keep me from my responsibilities." She raised her fist in the air. "I shall make up the time," she called and shook her fist for good measure. Then she took off in a sprint for her truck that Carl had left in the parking lot after he'd taken it off the lift.

"Don't speed," Carl yelled.

Ellie waved then jumped in the truck. She was pulling out of the lot as she slammed her door. A quick glance at the clock told her she should make the feed store her first stop. If she waited any later, the store would be packed. A fair amount of ranchers in the area liked to congregate around the feed store. So much so that a local woman started a food truck service specifically for them, giving the men even more reason to gather and talk trash. Ellie didn't want to get caught in that mess.

The day was shaping up to be sunny and warmer than the customary low-sixties May weather they usually had. Heat meant more men would be gossiping than working. She'd get her supplies and then head over to Williamses' ranch before heading home. Regardless of the sun, the bright and fun colors of the wild-flowers, or how she normally enjoyed watching old men gossip, Ellie wasn't feeling any of that today. She wanted to get home and have this day over as soon as possible.

The feed store was a mile south of Main Street and set off the road by a long drive. The wood building sat on a concrete slab with a wrap porch out front and four large bays in the back for loading trucks. Ellie drove to the back and pulled into the only empty bay, second from the end. She waved to the two ranchers parked to the right of her truck who were emptying pallets of feed onto their truck beds. She turned to the rancher on her left, and her hand froze mid-wave.

Dark stranger.

He was resting against the side of a shiny, brand-new looking, expensive black truck. No surprise there with the color choice. His back was against the passenger front side panel, his legs extended before him, and one foot crossed over the other. She caught the reflective glimpse of something silver around his neck.

Dog tags.

"What? I don't get a wave?" He gave a half smile that underlined his sarcastic question. He nodded to her tires. "Glad to see they're all inflated."

"I don't wave to strangers."

He pushed up from the truck and came toward her, arm extended, hand ready for a handshake. "I'm Shane Hannigan. My family owns the Wild Arrow Ranch. I think you might know my sister, Cricket."

It didn't take a brainiac to know that inside Shane Hannigan was power, passion, and a will of volcanic proportions. She'd felt it earlier today. He was the kind of guy she found sexy. From his physique, such as his strong jawline and broad shoulders, to the subtleties of his manliness heard in the timber of his voice. With trepidation, Ellie took his hand. "Ellie Greene."

As she expected, the moment her skin touched his, heat rushed through her palm and up her arm. He was danger, and she preferred men with an undercurrent that wouldn't make her life more complicated. That's why she avoided entanglements with men at all cost. She didn't have time for the ones she had to tell what to do, and she wasn't interested in being bossed around.

She pulled her hand away after two quick pumps of the arm. His eyes smoldered with the rapid current of energy inside him, waiting to break free. She didn't want to have anything to do with him. On some level, her Dad was the same. Willful, determined, and knew no boundaries. Look how that turned out for Ellie's mom. Living her life in a tent in some third-world country because her doctor husband wanted to change the world. That would not be Ellie's story. She would not give up her dream so another could live out theirs.

Ellie stepped to the bay door she'd parked by and pressed a buzzer.

"I know your grandma," he said and resumed his position back against his truck.

"Everyone does," she said and crossed her arms over her chest.

He glanced at her truck. "Any punctures in your tires?"

Ellie clenched her teeth. There was no denying she was unnerved. Strange things had been happening over the past few months, and Ellie really didn't want to admit out loud the occurrences weren't just coincidences. She knew better than that. No matter how hard she tried to deny it. And the last thing she wanted to do was talk about it with a stranger.

A stranger. Her mind caught on the thought. She'd seen him twice in one day. Unusual? Maybe not. "How long you been back in town?" Could there be a correlation?

"Top of three weeks," he said.

The flat tires had happened in the last two weeks. So it was possible Shane Hannigan from Broken Arrow Ranch was some kind of weirdo stalker and had set his eyes on her. Only, the other stuff started before that, and it was unlikely the incidents were separate. Or at least, she hoped they weren't. Two people causing her trouble was two people too many.

"I'm guessing Carl said there weren't any punctures," he said and crossed one foot over the other, relaxing.

She shook her head, then turned when the bay door behind her rolled up showing the inside of the feedstore storeroom.

"Hey Ellie," said Petey Clark. He was Burt the feedstore owner's youngest kid. Tall and so thin his natural posture was to curve forward at the shoulders, as if gravity were too much work.

Petey was one heck of a roper, though, a sport where he used his lankiness and length to his advantage.

"Hey, Petey, how are you?" She gave him a friendly swat on the shoulder. But not too hard lest she knock him over.

"Doing all right. How about you? How's Benny?" On occasion, Petey had come out to the farm to play with her goats.

"He's a handful. But I love him so," Ellie gushed. "Want me to help you load my order?"

Petey's brows furrowed. "I didn't see an order back there for you when I was prepping them. I thought it was strange. You always come on Tuesdays and Thursdays. Lemme go look again. Hang on." He shuffled away.

In the bay next to her, Colt, Burt's other son and almost identical in body shape to Petey, wheeled a trolley out to Shane. Ellie sat on her tailgate and waited for Petey.

"Here ya go, Shane. Your dad called in some extra stuff yesterday, and that's right here in this box." Travis pointed to a standard brown box that had the top cut off for easy access. He then handed Shane some papers and a pen.

Ellie watched the two of them load the large bags of feed into Shane's truck bed. He moved powerfully and easily and only occasionally did she see a slight grimace. It was hardly noticeable, and only seen by the slight wincing of his eyes. She wondered if it had to do with the foot he was favoring.

Petey came back looking confused. "There's nothing waiting for you. So I looked in the computer, and the order was canceled."

Ellie jumped off the tailgate. "Canceled? Who canceled it?"

Petey shrugged. "Looks like it was done online. Maybe your Grams did it? It was done through the farm account."

Ellie shook her head. "Why would Grams cancel food for the animals? It doesn't make any sense."

"Maybe you were hacked?" Petey suggested. "It happens on Facebook all the time."

Ellie couldn't figure it out. What she could no longer deny, though, was someone was harassing them. There were no two ways around it. "Petey, I need to feed the goats. I need my standard order. How soon can you get it together?"

Petey nodded. "I hear ya. That'll take me a while since I gotta get these orders done first." He gestured to the trucks at the bays and the two waiting in line. "This is our busy time."

"How soon?" Ellie bit her lip. She was already behind for the day. Grams was waiting at the farm stand for Ellie to relieve her. The farm ran like a well-oiled machine when there weren't any hurdles like today. Or over the past few weeks.

Petey scanned the parking lot. "Maybe an hour?"

Ellie shrugged and nodded. "Okay." What was she going to do? Say no? Pitch a fit? Though a fit sounded like a good idea. If only to burn off all her frustration.

Petey shuffled off, faster this time.

Ellie turned back to her truck to find Colt and Shane were done loading his truck. Colt walked back into the feed store. Shane was staring at her, his hands on his hips. He stepped up to her.

Shane said in a hushed voice, "Trust your gut, Ellie. Listen to what its saying. If it's telling you something's going down, then something's going down. If it's telling you not to trust me, don't trust me. If it's telling you not to trust someone else, listen to it. Go back and retrace everything that's happened. I'm guessing two flat tires with no screws in them and a canceled order of feed is not where it began. Try to find the beginning."

"But why—"

"You might not know the why until you know who. You might not know who until you know why. More than anything, you need to pay attention to your instincts. You get goose bumps around someone and feel uneasy? That's a warning. "

Ellie took in a shaky breath then blew it out slowly. She shook her head. "I can't imagine—"

He stepped closer and held up his hand. "Stop. That's called denial, and it can get you killed."

Fear ran through her, leaving her cold. "What do you know about it?" Panic had her taking it out on Shane. She instantly regretted being rude, but suddenly she didn't feel safe standing among the people she spent every day with. Shane was right. Someone was targeting her. Or the farm. Or maybe both.

He tapped her forehead. "Get out of there. You're talking yourself out of listening to your gut. I've spent my entire career staying alive because of my gut."

"Military, right?" Her eyes went to the chain at his neck. "Cricket's talked about you." Ellie wished she'd paid closer attention to the stories others had shared about the great Shane Hannigan. All she could recall was that there had been an explosion, and he'd been one of two survivors.

"Yeah, and had I not listened to my gut, I'd be dead right now instead of having this bum leg. Trust your instincts." He looked at something over her shoulder and took a step back. He whispered. "Trust no one." He raised his hand in a wave and called across the parking lot, "Good to see you, Mr. Landry."

Ellie turned to see the owner of their neighboring ranch to the northwest. The elder Landry, Lyle, ambled over to them. A lifelong rancher whose family started in the livestock business back when people drove wagons across the country. His ranch was the second biggest west of the Bighorn Mountains. Or it had been until the fire had taken half his herd and destroyed his grazing land. He was sun-dried, brittle around the edges, with skin tougher than leather and wrinkled like an elephant, but he had a confident air about him. Or he had. Now his shoulders were more stooped, his white hair thinning. He looked more tired than prominent. Ellie thought of him in a grandfatherly way, and her heart warmed when she saw him.

Lyle Landry stuck out his hand for Shane to shake. "Shane, thank you for your service. Very happy to see you're in one piece."

"Or two," Shane said. "Thank you. It's nice to have a break. Hoping I can get back into the thick of things sooner rather than later, in some capacity."

Ellie looked at Shane quizzically. His remark about two pieces was puzzling.

"If that's what you want," Mr. Landry said. "You can always stay here and plant some roots."

Shane shook his head. "Naw, no, sir. Not for me, yet. In due time."

"How's things going for you, Ellie, my girl?" asked Mr. Landry.

"My order was canceled. I'm waiting for Petey to get it together."

Mr. Landry's eyes narrowed. "What do you mean it was canceled?" Mr. Landry pulled an unlit cheroot from his back pocket and stuck it in his mouth, moving it around like a toothpick.

"Apparently, my account was hacked and whoever hacked it canceled my order." Ellie shrugged to show she didn't understand it any more than he did. Over his shoulder, she saw Norris Landry, Lyle's son, walking toward them. Ellie waved. He was her father's closest friend, had been since childhood, and they still kept in touch.

"We're loaded up, Pops," Norris said and clasped his father on the shoulder.

The elder Mr. Landry turned to his son. "Norris, someone hacked into Ellie's account. This kind of nonsense didn't happen in my day." He gave a shake of his head. "Sad how times have changed."

"That's awful," Norris said. He squeezed her shoulder in a comforting gesture. "What do you need us to do? We can help."

Ellie liked to watch Norris Landry. He reminded her of her father. Even though she was often irritated with her father, she still missed him. Norris filled that void. He was often on the farm helping her fix whatever wasn't working. Teaching her instead of doing it for her. Though he resembled his father, he was a softer version. Less sun had baked Uncle Norris's skin. His hands had seen less work.

Ellie wrapped her arms around herself. "Nothing. It's fixable. I just have to wait until Petey is free to put my order together."

Mr. Landry grunted and said between clenched teeth, his cheroot dangling precariously from his bottom lip. "When this feed store opened back in the forties, we used to load everything ourselves. Now it's like we can't be trusted to get our own supplies. Only pet food." He removed the cheroot and spit on the ground. "Ridiculous."

Shane agreed. "It sure would make things easier for Ellie if she didn't have to wait."

Uncle Norris chuckled. "Like clockwork, our Ellie. Must be driving you crazy to be off schedule."

Ellie's smile was slight. "More that I'm worried about Grams. I know she's fine, but I hate to think of her sitting at the farm stand all day."

Elder Landry resumed chewing his cheroot. "Let's do this. Norris will move our hay to your truck and off you go. We can wait for Petey."

Shane crossed his arms. "That's very generous."

Generous yes, thought Ellie. But now Shane had put disturbing thoughts into her head, and she suspected everyone. Even the Landrys. She'd grown up referring to Norris as her uncle, for Pete's sake. Was this a real act of kindness or were there ulterior motives?

"I can't let you do that. This day is shot anyway. What's another hour?" Ellie said, even though she wanted to take the hay.

"Another hour means you're working into the evening. I hear there's a coyote coming around to some of the ranches causing trouble. I'd feel better if I knew you weren't out too late," said the elder Landry.

"Your dad wouldn't like it either," Uncle Norris added. "Safety first."

Ellie didn't want to remind them she was often out late, either messing with the irrigation or hanging with the goats. She didn't run inside behind the safety of a door simply because the sun was setting. Working in Africa had helped hone her instincts, and Ellie was very confident her predator radar would ping if she were out and an animal were to come onto the farm.

Ellie conveniently ignored the fact that her radar hadn't pinged about predatory people.

"Pull your truck to ours, and I'll toss the bales over," Uncle Norris said as he began to walk to their truck.

Ellie did as he asked. Before she climbed into her truck, her gaze went to Shane's. He'd said his goodbye and was at his truck. His penetrating stare said everything.

Trust no one.

She nodded. She heard him loud and clear. Trouble was, trusting no one was easier said than done. She'd spent the last twelve years living, laughing, and sharing with the residents of Wolf Creek. She'd sat at their tables, made blankets for their babies, and brought many soup when they were sick. Ellie scanned the crowd. Someone was trying to intimidate her. To what end, she didn't know.

She pulled her truck alongside the Landrys' and got out to help move the hay over.

The elder Landry had caught Petey and was giving him the rundown on the change of plans.

When she was all loaded, she turned to the Landrys and said, "Thanks. Grams and I appreciate this. So do the goats."

Uncle Norris laughed. "Don't worry about it. You just make sure to tell Benny the Jet how I helped out and he can stop nipping at me from now on."

Ellie laughed, too, but she was thinking *trust no one.*

TUESDAY

Ellie left the feed store and headed out to Williamses' ranch to feed and water their cows. After the fire last summer and sudden loss of their livelihood, the Williams were heartbroken. Then by some fluke, natural gas was discovered on their property. The windfall of money gave them the opportunity to check off items on their bucket list. A rancher could be taken off the ranch, but ranching couldn't be taken out of the rancher.

Ellie's work was straightforward, and she finished quickly, spending a few extra minutes talking to the cows and rubbing their soft, velvety muzzles. The simplicity of the job allowed her racing thoughts to slow.

Dark Stranger Shane's warning made her uncomfortable. She was scared, and she didn't like it. She wished the solution was easy and she could blame Shane since he was new and a stranger to her. Logically, she knew accusing him didn't make a lot of sense, but the alternative was worse. One of her neighbors, possibly a trusted friend, was trying to scare her. Did they want to hurt her, too? What about Grams? Ellie's thoughts jumped from ominous ones to outright fear. She would go to her death protecting Grams.

Ellie had another problem. Shane Hannigan. He was the metaphoric red flag, and she was like a Barcelona bull—drawn to him. He had an energy and presence about him that was both annoying and intriguing. Oh how she loathed that her instincts told her he was safe, reliable, and honest. Her hormones told her he was sexy, probably really skilled with his hands, and a kisser that could stun a person into silence. His lips often captured her attention. Were they as soft as they appeared, or was that in contrast to his granite face that made them appear so kissable?

Ellie gave herself a mental slap upside the head. She didn't need one more distraction. She didn't need to get all wobbly-kneed over a guy who didn't want to be a farmer, who, for that matter, was just visiting. And she certainly didn't need him to swoop in and fix her problems. When it was time for Ellie Greene to take on a man, she would do it on her terms, and her terms only.

Ellie headed home, dark storm clouds rolling slowly in behind her. The hub of the farm, passed down from Greene to Greene, sat in the center of their substantial acreage. The two-story farmhouse was reached by traveling down a mile long drive. The large faded red barn was positioned out front, on the right side and perpendicular to the house. The previous years' crops used to sit behind the barn, but in the current rotation, the crops were now closer to the house, so behind the barn was a pasture. Pulling up to the house, she decided to check in with Grams before going straight to the barn and goat pen. "Grams, I'm back," Ellie called and walked through the house. She bit her lip in worry. She was overreacting, but as soon as she saw her grandmother, she would feel better.

Ellie found Grams sitting in the family room at the back of the house. Stretched out in her recliner, she was knitting. Her long silver hair was braided and wrapped in a bun at the nape of her neck and she was dressed in worn jeans and a sweatshirt. Ellie rarely saw Grams in anything else but comfortable. Grams was whistling, and Ellie knew everything was okay. She let out the breath she was holding.

"Grams," Ellie said and came to stand in front of her. Grams's hearing aids were on the table beside her.

Minnie Greene startled, her hand going to her chest. "You surprised me."

"If you'd wear your hearing aids, you would have heard me come in. What if I was a bad guy? Someone could sneak up on you." Ellie had to raise her voice or else Grams would only hear murmuring.

Grams waved her off. "Who would be out here and want to hurt an old lady?" She pointed to the small earpieces with her knitting needles. "You know I hate those things. They buzz all the time."

"If you took them to the hearing aid place, they could fix that." This was not a new conversation, but it was an easy one. She needed to tell Grams her suspicions about being a target, but she dreaded scaring the older woman.

"You're late," Grams said and tucked her needles into her yarn. She reached for one of the hearing aids and fiddled with inserting it.

"I had a few problems."

"What sort of problems?" Minnie clicked a button, and a high-pitched squeal came from her ear. Both women winced until Minnie was able to adjust it. "These stupid, cheap pieces of sh—"

Ellie cut her off. "Grams, they do the job." And they weren't cheap. They were stupid expensive and, personally, Ellie thought seniors were being price gouged by hearing aid companies.

"Have you had lunch?" Grams asked while she inserted the other one.

"Not yet. I'm going to unload the feed and go see the goats."

She glanced at her watch. "If I wait a few hours, I can just skip lunch and go straight to dinner. A storm is rolling in, too."

"I'll make you a light snack then," Grams said and pushed from the recliner with a grunt.

Ellie squeezed her Grams hand as she passed, then headed out. She walked briskly across the yard to the old barn, faded to a dull red. Once used to sort and store large volumes of crops, the barn was far bigger than what they needed for their current state of operations. It was part housing for the horses and a llama, part storage and staging for crops, and part shop for her latest endeavors to make money. Ellie had converted a portion to make soaps and lotions. Eventually, when time allowed, she'd add balms, salves, and bath fizzes to her products. But that dream felt out of reach these last few weeks.

The front of the barn faced an unfenced, unused meadow that turned more arid and rocky the further south the land traveled toward Wind River Reservation. The fenced yard for the animals started two-thirds down the left side of the barn and stretched around the backside of the large building. This area housed the goats' pen and allowed them to run and play. She'd even built them an obstacle course of sorts with ramps and called it Goat-landia. Their "house" abutted the left side of the barn. The fenced area had two access points. The first was a gate on the opposite side of the barn, closer to the farmhouse. The second required walking though the barn and out the back door, which opened into the fenced area. Ellie chose the latter because she needed to unload her truck and feed the goats while she was at it. She left the front double doors of the barn open, but made sure to close the back door when she walked out. Her goats were sneaky little buggers, and escaping was their favorite pastime.

Goatlandia was quiet. Too quiet. Even though a storm was rolling in, Ellie expected to find at least one or two goats outside. Run Around Sue was a daring fawn-colored, ninja-like pygmy goat and lacked response inhibition. She could always be found zipping around the yard. That was, after all, how she got her name. Even with both front legs casted Run Around Sue exhibited a level of energy that was exhausting to watch. She'd run in circles, bouncing off other goats and structures until she'd fall over, lay on her side panting for a few minutes, catch her breath and then would jump up and repeat the activity. She especially loved to pick on Bad Bad Leroy Brown, an all-brown Nigerian, since he'd always give chase.

The yard was empty. Ellie stuck her head inside the pen. Eight goats lay inside, huddled together. Ellie counted heads again, thinking she'd miscounted. Dolly the llama was also missing. Ellie stepped away and whistled shrilly before calling out the animal's names. A sense of unease crept up her spine as she tried to figure out where the llama and Benny were.

She'd taken in Dolly over a year ago to convalesce as a favor to Bryce, and she was nowhere to be seen. Dolly, a laid-back creature, had gotten injured when she'd become territorial with another llama and wanted to play put-up-your-dukes. Unaware of the fence separating Dolly from the other llama, she'd gotten her front hooves stuck and severely cut. Her owners had been irresponsible and let the cuts get infected. That's why Ellie was rehabbing Dolly. Though, truth be told, rehab was long over and Dolly was now part of their family. Ellie knew the llama was never going to leave. Her owners had turned Dolly over when they realized her vet bills would be over twenty-five bucks. Dolly had never strayed from the yard or tangled with a fence since.

Ellie paused to look for movement, and that's when she heard the mewling. Ellie turned in a circle, searching. Her heart raced with alarm. Wind whipped through the yard, and Ellie stopped short. The wind caught the far gate and pushed it wide. It banged closed and bounced open again.

How did the gate get freed? Were her little guys running loose somewhere?

Ellie tried to stamp down her rising panic and keep her cool.

She heard the mewling again, but it was in the wind, not coming from the goat pen like she'd initially thought. Ellie scanned the grazing field beyond the yard. Far behind the barn, at least half a football field length away, she spotted Dolly, her head bent forward, gently nudging a jumbled mound of something indistinguishable on the ground. Suddenly, Ellie's brain processed what she was seeing. Benny's cart, the device he used to help him walk, was upturned. The lightning bolts painted on the side faced the wrong direction. One little hoof stuck out.

"Benny!" she hopped the fence, saying a silent prayer of thanks they hadn't had the money to make it electric. Ellie sprinted through the yard, making her way to him as fast as she could. Her heart beat so loudly she almost didn't hear her grandmother call her name.

She turned to see Grams loping across the yard as fast as her aging hips could take her, a shotgun in her hand.

"He's been attacked. Check on the other animals," Ellie cried as she reached Benny and fell to her side, coming in on a slide. Instantly, she saw the tears in his shoulder and hindquarters. With shaky but deft fingers, she began to undo his harness and free him from his walker. Dolly, relinquishing her job as sentry, backed away, not a fan of human contact. Ellie appreciated the space the llama was giving. Benny was alive because Dolly had likely gone after the animal that had done this.

A coyote. It had to be.

"It's going to be okay, baby. Momma's here." She kissed the bridge of his nose and stroked it gently while sliding the harness down his body and off his back legs. She cradled the back legs so they wouldn't flop to the ground. When Benny was born, he'd been trampled by another larger goat. The damage to his back legs had rendered them useless. Once free, Ellie took off her shirt and wrapped Benny in it.

He mewled, his eyes closed.

Ellie caught herself mid-sob and forced herself to buck up. She could fall apart later. She cradled him against her and rushed from the field, trying not to jostle him.

"Everyone else is okay," Grams called from the goat pen. "You go. I'll get Dolly."

Though seconds, maybe a full minute, passed before Ellie made it to her truck, the time felt like an eternity. She continued to coo sweet words of comfort to Benny. Inside the truck, she simultaneously called Bryce and floored the gas, Benny in her lap, his breathing rapid and shallow.

5

TUESDAY

S hane drove to his parents' ranch with his mind on Ellie. His gut was sounding an alarm about her situation. Someone was harassing her, that was clear. What was less clear for her, downright murky even, was who it might be. He hoped his words of warning were enough to spur her into action. She needed to protect herself. Knowing she might not was unsettling. He considered sitting outside her farm to provide an extra set of eyes, but that seemed extreme. After all, he didn't know her, and he hadn't been invited to do surveillance. His actions could be misconstrued.

Shane grunted in frustration. One more situation where he was tits on a bull. This new trend in his life was irritating the hell outta him. He was gonna need some action soon or else he might lose his mind.

Shane drove down the windy road that led to Wild Arrow Ranch. Surrounded by numerous pines, the ten-thousand-acre cattle ranch was part forest and part pasture. A hundred yards behind the main house, a stone and wood ranch, stood two large umber-colored barns. Shane veered right onto a side road that would take him to the barns and circumvent the house. A glance at the sky told him a storm was rolling in, and he wanted to unload the feed before it hit.

When he came around the side of the barn he caught sight of Bryce Jacobson's truck. Shane and Bryce, the local vet, had graduated high school together and had been just as good friends back then as they were now. Shane parked alongside the larger of the two weathered barns and entered through a side door.

Shane found Bryce in the stall with a mare due to foal. He rested his arm along the rail of the stall door and looked in. "How's she doing?"

"Getting close. Not swelling yet, so we've got some time." Bryce rubbed his hand down the mare's neck. "Cricket called last night looking for you."

Shane grunted his irritation. "She told me. The parents called her looking for me. Did Hannah say anything?"

Bryce chuckled. "What can she say? I didn't tell her what you were up to. How'd it go?"

Shane thought about all the work he'd done last night and nodded. "Not too bad. By the end of the night, I could stay on for four seconds at full force. But damn if my legs don't ache."

Bryce was the only one who knew Shane had connected with an old friend with access to a mechanical bull. Shane was "training" on it every chance he got. He wasn't looking to get into broncing bulls; he just wanted to improve his overall strength, particularly in his bum leg. He didn't want his injury to become a hindrance by any definition. Afterward, disappointed he hadn't felt the jubilee he'd expected for riding the bull as long as he did, Shane had kicked off a pity party with just him and his friend, Jose Cuervo.

Bryce fist-bumped him. "That's pretty good. I think my best time is five."

"Yeah, well, you're a sissy. Always worried about whiplash and—"

"Because it's real," Bryce argued. "The only thing I like scrambled are my eggs. You gonna tell your parents?"

"Hell no. Can you imagine the flack I'd get? Mom worries enough as it is. They wouldn't see this as rehab, but insanity."

"Well, you need a cover. Or something else to fill your time." Bryce let himself out of the stall and started packing his medical bag.

"I'm hesitant to tell Cricket because she'll worry, too."

Bryce finished and stood next to him, arms crossed over his chest. He was built much like Shane, tall with broad shoulders that were honed from working with large animals, swinging ropes over their heads, and chucking bales of hay off a truck. His dark hair was curly but cut close, and he sported a dimple in each cheek that, prior to marriage, he'd used as a device to enchant chicks. "You heard from the Marines yet?"

Shane shook his head. Being a man without a place to belong was hard. He needed to be somewhere with a purpose. This state of in-between left him feeling restless. "Let's be honest." He tapped his bum leg. "They ain't keeping me in my job with this injury. I'm not sure I want to know what the alternative offer will be."

Bryce leaned against the wall of the stall. "I was talking to Fort Besingame. He's the new sheriff. You remember him, right? He used to spend summers here."

"Yeah, I think so."

"He was saying Game and Fish is looking for a sharpshooter to help with some wildlife control issue. They've been looking for a warden for the area for over a year but will settle for a sharpshooter. Seems like we might have a coyote or a mountain lion that might have rabies. I thought of you. You're an excellent tracker, and you've been trained to be a Marine Sniper. Seems like this job was made for you," Bryce said.

"Except for this." Shane stomped his foot.

Bryce rolled his eyes. "Except what? You just spent last night working out on a mechanical bull. I don't see anything holding you back."

"I haven't been home for the last ten years. Except for Laura's funeral. I don't know this town anymore."

"Excuses," Bryce said.

"Prime example, take this Ellie Greene. Where did she come from?" Shane crossed his arms over his chest and shifted the weight off his injured leg.

Bryce smiled. "She came from the loins of Paul Greene, Minnie's son. He's some doctor spending his life working in third-world countries. Ellie is one of my favorite people. Hands down."

"So she's not crazy?" Shane didn't think she was but had to ask. Maybe she was one of those attention-seeking sorts.

Bryce startled. "Crazy? No, why would you say that?" He studied Shane. Then gave a start, his mouth dropping open slightly. "Oh, I see."

Shane shook his head and pushed off the stall door. "No, you don't see. Don't make something out of nothing."

"Oh, sure, it's nothing. Then why did you ask about her? She's pretty cute, right? Not that I'm looking. I only have eyes for Hannah, but Ellie's got those killer green eyes." Bryce chuckled.

Yeah, they were killer, and her curly hair, wound so tight like tiny corkscrews, made him want to wrap a strand around his finger while he caressed her cheek. Yeah, he'd been hit with that desire while at the feed store. He might have taken a hit on the head when he got tossed from the mechanical bull last night. That could explain his current fascination with Ellie. He had no need for a woman in his life right now. His present situation was jacked up. He couldn't see jacking up hers, too. Not now when she was already having problems.

"I think someone is harassing her," Shane said.

Bryce's expression said he thought Shane was nuts. "Why? Who? What the hell are you talking about?"

Shane told him about the tire and the feed store. "Anything else weird happening?"

"I'll have to think about it. Nothing's coming to mind. The farm is struggling, but lots of others are, too."

"Anyone you can think of who might do this?" Shane knew the answer before he asked. Unless the person were walking around telling everyone what they were doing, no one would know who was causing Ellie her troubles.

Bryce shook his head. "It could be anyone. I can ask Fort if anyone else is having troubles. Maybe he'll know something."

Shane grimaced. "Doubtful."

"I can't imagine anyone who would want to hurt Ellie or Minnie. But I'll keep my eyes peeled." Bryce reached for his bag but stopped short when his phone rang. He pulled it from his back pocket and glanced at the screen before showing it to Shane.

"Speak of the devil." He pressed the talk button. "Hey Ell's, what's up?" Instantly Bryce's posture stiffened, and he cut his eyes to Shane. "Calm down. Tell me, where he's hurt?"

Shane grabbed Bryce's vet bag and started walking to the exit, Bryce behind him. When his friend snapped his fingers, Shane turned to see him pointing at traps hanging on the wall. Their purpose was to catch wildlife stalking the herd.

"Okay, I'm on my way to the office. I'll meet you there. Just keep pressure on the wound. Breathe Ellie." He disconnected and turned to Shane. "Coyote got into their pen and attacked one of her goats. Grab a gun. Once I'm done with being a vet, I'm going out to hunt this thing, and I could use your help."

"I'll be seconds behind you," Shane said and tossed the medical bag to his friend.

He jogged to the house to get a rifle from his father and to briefly apprise them of the situation, ignoring the tiny ache in his knee from the pounding run. Maybe he had overdone it last night.

Cricket stepped out the side door. "What's happened?" she called.

"Ellie just called Bryce. Seems one of her goats was attacked by a coyote." He pushed past her as he spoke. The pain in his knee flared to brilliant and sharp pain.

"Oh, no," Cricket said. "I'm going to help, too."

When she grabbed his arm, he paused in his single-minded focused to get the shotgun and looked at her.

"I don't like this, Shane. Not at all."

Neither did he. His instincts vibrated, transmitting a warning. Something wasn't right.

6

TUESDAY

The vet clinic sat on several acres and included pastures, dog runs, and a corral. The building itself was a simple square shape and, inside, the waiting room, restroom, and front desk were stationed at the front of the space. The exam rooms, kennels, lab, and surgical unit, all hidden behind double swinging doors, filled the remaining two-thirds of the space.

Standing near the front desk, Sabrina Holloway didn't move to turn on all the clinic lights, letting the few Hannah had left on when she closed the clinic suffice. The bright lights would highlight the blood on Ellie's clothes and no one needed to see that, especially not Ellie.

Sabrina studied the scared woman sitting in the plastic chair. "Defeated" summed her up perfectly. Life had taken a chunk out of Ellie Greene. A large one. If her little goat died, Sabrina wasn't sure how the woman would cope. She looked to be barely hanging on as it was. And not just now, scared for her pet, but earlier at the diner.

Sabrina was in the business of knowing people, sussing them out to ascertain what they needed from life. She wasn't a psychiatrist, but a matchmaker, and being the daughter of a millionaire con man who gambled for fun had taught her at an early age how to understand people, their needs, and what drove them.

Ellie Greene was a woman in need of something. Sabrina was not so single-minded to assume it was love. Right now Ellie needed reassurance about her beloved pet's well-being. But there was something missing. A spark, perhaps? Maybe the ability to laugh or let go? Or perhaps it was something more primitive, to know she had a value.

Movement from the double swinging doors that led back to Bryce's surgical and treatment rooms caught Sabrina's eye. Looking through one of the small windows in the door was Shane. Like a starburst in her mind's eye, Sabrina experienced an *a-ha* moment. What was missing in Ellie was also gone in Shane, too. Perhaps his had been blown out of him when the IED had exploded on a barren street in Afghanistan and took out the Humvee Shane was in.

He watched Ellie, his brow drawn inward giving him an angry, menacing look. He wasn't angry with Ellie, but her circumstances. He'd said as much when he and Bryce had come charging into the office. It was in his fury, Sabrina saw the hint of something. Fire perhaps? An ember, burning deep inside him that was begging to be stoked.

Sabrina and Cori had come to Hannah's for lunch to distract Cori from her impending labor and delivery. Cricket had arrived moments behind Shane. She'd seen the spark in him, too, and cast a knowing look in Sabrina's way. Sabrina had answered with a barely perceivable nod. Yes, there was something here. Something between Shane and Ellie. Or maybe only Shane. Sabrina would know soon enough.

Shane and Ellie weren't like Sabrina's typical clients. The people Sabrina matched were strangers who knowingly entered into an arranged marriage for a plethora of reasons. But what

Shane and Ellie did have in common with Sabrina's other clients was their lack of hope.

Defeated was synonymous with hopelessness, and currently Sabrina didn't know two people more hopeless than Shane and Ellie.

Sabrina Holloway had an idea.

7

TUESDAY

Ellie shifted sideways in the uncomfortable folding chair in Bryce's waiting area. She clutched her hands, stained with Benny's blood, in her lap. She squeezed them together, her skin sticking to itself, in an attempt to be patient. Across from her were the empty front desk and the double swinging doors. Benny was back there. She stared, riveted, looking for movement behind those doors. The clinic was quiet. Only the occasional bark of a kenneled dog breaking the silence led Ellie to believe that someone was on the move back there. Each time she'd sit up and wait for Bryce to come through the doors. He hadn't done so yet.

Cricket and Cori's friend—the woman's name escaped Ellie—came in. Cricket stood over Ellie. "Come on," she said and held out her hand, "let's get you cleaned up."

She led Ellie to the restroom and stood outside while Ellie scrubbed the patches of dried blood from her hands. Remnants of Benny's trauma were seen in the few streaks down her face where she must have wiped away her tears. A round, reddish-brown patch the size of a small fist was center on her T-shirt above her waistline. Ellie couldn't stand to see herself any longer and left the room.

"How you holding up?" Cricket asked, rubbing her hands up and down Ellie's back as they walked together to the waiting chairs.

"Okay," Ellie said and glanced at the doors separating her from Benny before sitting back in the dreaded chair.

"Ellie, you remember Sabrina Holloway? She's Cori's friend from Texas."

Ellie glanced at the other woman and nodded, vaguely recalling their first introduction, her attention more on what was happening in the surgical suite. Cricket sat beside her, Sabrina next to Cricket.

Sabrina leaned forward, a soft smile on her face. "Fort will be here in a sec to ask you some questions. Are you up for that?"

Ellie shrugged. "I suppose. I'm not sure what good it can do. I wasn't there." Enter guilt. For every minute she had no info about Benny, she spent retracing her steps and damning herself for not being there to protect or help him. She cursed her flat tire. She cursed the delay at the feed store. Had she been on schedule, maybe this wouldn't have happened.

The shuffle-step of boots coming her way drew her attention away from her guilt. When Shane pushed through the double doors, Ellie wanted to run to him. Even hide behind him, if only for a moment. His presence alone was slowly infusing strength into her. It might not be true, but it felt as if Shane was watching her back.

He stood before her and held up his hands in front of him in defense, appearing to already know she was going to ask him a million questions. "I don't know anything, yet," he said, cutting Ellie off before she could ask.

Sabrina said, "I was wondering if there was anything I could do to help?"

Ellie shook her head.

Shane shuffled over and sat beside her. "I wasn't back with Bryce. I was back there getting gear ready."

"Ready for what?" Ellie asked, her gaze on the double doors.

"We're prepping to hunt this animal down."

Ellie bent forward, rested her chest against her legs, and wrapped her arms under them. She faced Shane, closed her eyes, and said quietly, "Remember when you told me to trust my instincts?"

He grunted in acknowledgment.

"I think someone did this on purpose." Her voice broke as she admitted her fears out loud. She sucked in a ragged breath and opened her eyes. They locked with his. "I haven't had a chance to inspect, but the gate to the goats pen looked broken. I'd latched it earlier this morning when I fed the goats, and it was fine then."

Shane asked, "Any chance it was loose or not in the best condition?" His voice was soft and not accusatory.

"No," Ellie said weakly. "It's a newer gate. I had to get it when I decided to rehab Dolly."

"I can vouch for the quality of the gate and it being locked," Cricket said. "I was there this morning and went out to see the goats."

Surprised, Ellie sat up and faced Cricket. "You were at the farm?"

Cricket's smile was also part grimace. "I was out there asking your grandmother if Cori and I could do an article on the goats."

"Why didn't you just ask me at the diner?" Ellie had, after all, seen Cricket and the others there this morning.

Cricket looked embarrassed. "I didn't think of it until after you left. Sorry. When I got there, your grandma was working the farm stand. We talked a bit, and then she told me to go on to the house to see the goats. I did. I entered through the back gate because I parked by the house and not the barn."

"All the goats were in the yard?" Ellie asked.

Cricket nodded. "Dolly, too. The gate latch was solid. It took both hands for me to open it, and when I closed it, I made sure it caught."

Shane asked, "Did you leave the same way?"

Cricket shook her head. "I went through the barn."

"The barn had been secure when I went through to find the goats," Ellie said wearily, putting her head back on her knees, an ache searing her middle. "Cricket didn't leave the gate unlatched. It's designed to swing closed behind and latch on impact. Before I saw Benny, I noticed the wind was pushing the gate open and the latch wasn't catching." When she pictured Benny's cart on its side, tears welled up in her eyes.

"Who would break a gate so little goats could get hurt? And special needs goats at that?" Her voice broke on a sob. Ellie let the tears flow, her jeans absorbing the drops. Cricket rubbed her back as she continued. "Whoever did this wanted any one or number of my animals to get hurt. But they had to know my special needs goats would be the likely target. How could they not be? Run Around Sue has two prostheses. Benny doesn't have use of his back legs. He uses a walker!" Ellie continued to hug herself.

The others sat in silence while Ellie collected herself.

When she thought she'd regained some semblance of control, Ellie sat up and blew out a breath. "I want to find out who is doing this to us and make that person pay," Ellie said. She glanced up at Shane.

He nodded. "Let's start with looking for the coyote. A few of the other ranchers have had some trouble, and Fort was here when you brought your goat in—"

"He was picking up Cori," Cricket supplied.

Shane continued, "He asked if he could hire me to hunt this coyote. It's not common for a coyote to hunt so early in the day. I took the job. I'll get this animal, Ellie. Don't you worry."

Ellie shook her head, "But what about the person who is doing this to me? I've been thinking about it. My flat tire yesterday put me off schedule by thirty minutes. And that's because I have a spare tire handy. Today with the flat and the feed store mix-up, I was nearly delayed two hours. Everyone who knows Grams and me knows that when she closes the farm stand she goes to the house. Everyone also knows she's hard of hearing."

"I wonder if the first flat tire was a test to see how long it would delay you?" Cricket posed.

"What time does she close the farm stand?" Shane asked.

"Eleven," Cricket and Ellie said in unison.

Ellie gestured to Cricket. "See, everyone knows that."

"In the summer they stay open later," Cricket added.

Ellie gestured at Cricket again. What she'd said only further proved Ellie's point.

"I have a suggestion, and I want you to both hear me out before you say no," Sabrina said.

Ellie straightened. She wasn't sure this was going to be good. Not with a start like that.

Sabrina continued, leaning forward and speaking softly, "I think Shane needs to be a presence here at the farm. The two of you need to work together to figure this out. As I see it, what's happening is one of two scenarios. Either someone is paying a person to do these things to you, Ellie, in which case Shane's presence will put him off—"

"How so?" Ellie asked.

"No offense, Ellie, but you're easy money. What's been happening to you has taken little work and ingenuity. If a person was hired to do this, its been quick cash for them. They'll keep doing it, too, so long as it stays easy. With Shane around, that complicates things, and the job no longer becomes easy money."

"So all this could stop?" Ellie asked then rolled her eyes. "All this because a man is hanging around."

Sabrina shrugged as if to say "it is what it is."

"And the other scenario?" Cricket asked.

Sabrina grimaced. "Either way, it's obvious whoever is doing this to you knows you. If they haven't hired a person, then they're doing it themselves."

Ellie struggled to connect the dots. "And having Shane around stops that how?"

Sabrina smiled softly. "This is where it gets tricky. Since it's likely a local, the person knows Shane. Knows he doesn't need money so he can't be bought—"

"Damn right," Shane said. "They'll also know I will tear them apart."

"Well," Cricket said, "the problem is you're not staying here forever. So this person might just wait you out."

Shane harrumphed his displeasure.

Sabrina said, "Unless you can make them think there's something between you and Ellie that might make you stay. Say, perhaps, a blooming love?"

Ellie groaned and dropped her head in her hands. "You want me to pretend to like him? And him to like me? How embarrassing." Heat rushed to her face.

Sabrina nodded. "Making it look like you two are interested in each other might smoke this person out. We make it look like Shane's invested in you and the farm, and it complicates everything for this person. Any chance you could have a disgruntled ex doing this? If so, that's another reason to pretend to have a new man around."

Ellie popped up out of her chair, not caring her humiliation was likely making her the shade of a beet, and spun to face them. "Until they get word that Shane's out of here. So all we've really done is delayed things."

"Maybe," Shane said, his voice calm. "Maybe not. Maybe in the time I'm hanging out with you, we can figure out who is doing this and put a stop to it."

"And we'll just keep any of Shane's future plans on the down low. It stays in this group." Cricket swirled her finger to those sitting there. "Bryce, Hannah, Cori, and Fort included."

"That's a lot of people," Ellie said, her arms akimbo.

"Yeah, but one is the sheriff. That's not a bad thing," Cricket pointed out.

Ellie sighed deeply. She didn't have to think about what they were proposing. Seeing Benny on the ground was catalyst enough to know she needed to take immediate action, drastic as it might be. Heck, they could've proposed darn near anything, and she would have accepted as long as it meant someone was helping her. Animals were getting hurt. Were people next? Ellie would never be able to live with herself if another being were hurt because she was too proud to ask for help. Holding the trembling goat in her lap on the drive over had been catalyst enough. Yes, Ellie loved her independence, but not if it meant she had to be selfish, too. She would take any help she could get.

She turned to Shane and studied him. "What is it you do in the Marines?" Why had this dark stranger been the first person to clue into something amiss in her life? Who was he outside of Cricket's brother?

"I'm a Marine recon sniper." He returned her stare with a steady one of his own.

Ellie nodded. She wasn't sure what a Marine recon sniper meant, but the words themselves told her a lot. He was not only dangerous but knew a lot about danger as well. Earlier she'd promised herself to avoid Shane; now she had to pretend to be dating him.

Bryce came through the double doors.

Ellie forgot what she was thinking and rushed to meet him. "Benny?" She whispered the question.

Bryce pulled off a surgical cap and held it in his hands. "He's going to be okay. He'll need to be sedated for a while, and I'll keep him here for a few days to make sure everything is healing like it should. He's a trooper."

Ellie tucked her head to gather her emotions. She wanted to drop to her knees and sob with relief. When she'd gained an ounce of composure, she asked, "Will he be able to walk?" Benny's back legs might not work, but now she worried about the front. The injuries to his front leg and shoulder had looked gruesome.

"Yeah, he had more puncture wounds than anything. There was some tearing, but nothing that won't heal properly. He's lucky. I'm not sure why the attacking animal didn't... "

"Dolly," Ellie said. "I think Dolly saved his life. She was standing next to him when I found him."

Bryce smiled, "Good ol' Dolly llama. Smartest thing I did was bring her to you." He reached out and rubbed her shoulder. "I'll give you five minutes with Benny, and then I want you to go home. Try to rest. Come back tomorrow and spend some time with Benny when he's alert."

Ellie nodded. Shane shifted beside her, and she looked at him. She despised the idea of needing help, that she alone wasn't enough, but conversely was grateful he would be there. Because if she had to pick someone from town to help her, who would she choose?

"What's it going to be?" he asked.

Ellie stuck her hands in the front pockets of her jeans and let her shoulders slump. She'd been determined to run this ranch without help. Sure, the occasional kindness of a fellow rancher or farmer lending their expertise was neighborly, not codependence. But Ellie was in over her head. She wasn't a cop, much less a detective. Stubborn was what she was. But this wasn't just about her.

She blew out her cheeks. "Okay, but only because innocent animals are being targeted. What if this person goes after Grams next? I can't bear the thought. Come over in the afternoon, and we'll set things in motion." Ready to see Benny, she stepped away toward Bryce.

"You working at the diner in the morning?" Shane asked.

Ellie nodded.

"Then I'll be there. What time do you go in?"

"Four."

He fidgeted with the large complicated watch at his wrist. "It's set. I'll meet you there at four. We'll go from there."

Ellie nodded again, feeling a bit childish for not having more to say. But she was numb and exhausted and desperately wanted to see her little goat. She faced Bryce but didn't have to ask. He gestured for her to follow him.

She took two steps and realized Shane was right behind her. "You're coming, too?"

His face was devoid of emotion. "Consider me your shadow. Where you go, I go."

Why did those words comfort and frighten her simultaneously?

SABRINA AND CRICKET stood at the large window in Bryce's waiting room and watched Shane walk Ellie to her truck and then jog to his. They'd barely spent five minutes with the little goat, and Shane had forced her out the door to head home. Sabrina waited until both trucks were out of the parking lot before speaking.

"Good cover about the newspaper article," she said.

Cricket turned to her with a wide smile. "Like that? I came up with that on the fly. Of course, now, I have to actually do an article, which is fine. Its a good human interest piece."

"You could have said something like you were there to get lotion or something. Didn't you say Ellie makes great goat milk body lotion?"

Cricket slapped her forehead. "That would have been so much easier." She leaned toward Sabrina conspiratorially and lowered her voice. "Minnie Greene is on board. She'll do what she can to help us with these two. I told her we thought they'd make a lovely couple, and she agreed."

Sabrina clasped her hands together in happiness. "They won't need a whole lot of pushing. I've never seen two people who needed each other more." Sabrina paused. "Well, this week I haven't."

She and Cricket laughed.

Cricket tilted her head to the side in thought and sighed. "When we conspired to bring these two together, making Shane Ellie's knight in shining armor, I pictured him helping her with some of her work, doing odd jobs around the ranch. I never imagined he might truly come to her rescue." She shook her head in disbelief. "Now, I'm even more thankful Shane will be looking out for Ellie, and even Grams. I'm worried about them."

"What's happening is troublesome, indeed." Sabrina agreed.

Cricket said, "I hope this works. I hope we haven't made a bad situation worse."

Sabrina nodded. "They both deserve some happiness. Even if it's only temporary."

8

WEDNESDAY

E llie made it home slightly after midnight. Grams had fallen asleep on the couch while waiting for her. Ellie relayed Benny's status then ushered Grams to bed with a promise to talk more thoroughly when the sun was up.

How much should Ellie tell her? How would she explain Shane's presence? Grams was no fool, but she'd also had a rough few years. She didn't need any more stress. With Gramps passing, her hearing decreasing, and Ellie's father, Grams's only child, a huge disappointment in the help department, Ellie and this farm were all Grams had. Telling her someone was trying to sabotage one or both of those would not go over well.

Ellie considered reaching out to her father but nothing would come of it. She knew what his response would be. He'd say that Grams and Ellie's problems were first world. That Ellie should return to mission work with them, and Grams should move to Florida to live with her sister. Two things neither Ellie nor Grams wanted. Helping others in third-world countries was admirable. No question about it. But Grams and Ellie were at risk of losing everything, including the farm. That didn't feel very first world as far as problems went.

Bringing in Shane was a no-brainer. At the very least, his presence might stem the flow of all the money Ellie had to clean up the messes from whoever was harassing her. Ellie didn't have extra funds and was constantly robbing Peter to pay Paul. Of course, Ellie couldn't tell anymore what was a typical farm expense because of wear and tear or purposeful damage. In addition to fixing all the truck flats, they had broken irrigation systems, products stolen from the farm stand, replaced old fencing, and now the gate lock.

Right now, she and Grams were being nickeled and dimed to the farm's demise.

Ellie shuffled to the bathroom, desperate to fully wash Benny's blood off her. The yellow light flickered dimly in the old farmhouse bath with its claw foot tub and shower curtain that encircled it. The hardwood boards were worn in spots, bowing in others where water leaks had penetrated and warped the floor. Ellie set the running water to hot and sat on the tub's edge, waiting. The old pipes needed time to get moving. The old water heater was slow, too.

Ellie had so many great ideas for the farm. Such as starting a community supported agriculture account, or CSA, and opening an online store to sell their goat's milk products and her hand-sewn goods. But all that required time and extra money to buy supplies. What little product they made, they sold. The farm stand rarely had extras. So upping the game was a smart move. Or so Ellie had thought, but when she and Grams had made their plan, that's when the universe began to thwart it.

If it wasn't for Mr. Phillips's support, the rancher south of them, Ellie wasn't sure they'd have made it this far. He had fixed for free the pipes in the house, the crop irrigation system, rotten wood pieces on the porch, and fences. Never mind the free meat he'd often provided in exchange for some of their veggies.

Ellie stuck her hand under the shower spray, testing the heat. She dragged her tired bones to stand under the spray. She felt far older than her twenty-eight years.

Failure did that to a person.

Losing this farm would be one more dark mark against her. Having failed out of nursing school for poor grades, then quit working on an education degree one year into it, and finally skipped out on her parents and their missionary work without so much as a see-ya-later, losing this farm would cinch it. Ellie would be a consummate loser. An epic failure. Hopeless.

Those thoughts trampling through her mind sparked an anger within her. She seethed as she scrubbed at the dried blood on her stomach and the rest of her body.

If having Shane's help meant the farm would survive, Ellie would accept that. Sure, she'd envisioned herself being the savior. She'd pictured the success and accolades being all hers. She'd dreamt of telling her parents about how she turned around the farm, how she found a way to make it sustainable.

Ellie finished washing and stepped from the tub, steam swirling around her. She toweled off quickly then rushed to her room to dress in the worn long johns she used for pajamas. How many nights had she fantasized about telling her parents about her success? Countless, that's how many. Ellie wanted this farm to survive. Ellie wanted to carry along her family's tradition of being farmers. She loved her life here. Try as she might, she couldn't picture herself doing anything other than sewing, creating products, walking the crops, planting seeds, and raising these silly goats. What would she do if she didn't have all this? Who would she be?

Ellie sank into her bed and sighed heavily from exhaustion, both mental and physical. She slid between the sheets and pulled the patchwork quilt up to her chin, then she pressed her palms to her eyes and let the tears flow from between the cracks.

SHANE MADE it to Cricket's house a few minutes after she did. First, he'd followed Ellie home to make sure she got there safely. He'd been sorely tempted to sleep in his truck and stake out the place, but he needed a game plan. Time and effort were not commodities he liked to waste. Tomorrow they would coordinate efforts and go from there.

He fell onto the bed in his sister's guest room and stretched. His body was humming with anticipation. Finally, he had a task, one he wanted, and he couldn't wait to get to it. This was the adrenaline high he missed. Being a sniper in the Marines meant life was full of these highs, and he was the first to admit he was a junkie in that aspect. Getting back into the game, tame as this one was, was what he'd been craving.

Spending time with cute-face Ellie wasn't going to be a hardship either. He liked her hard outer shell. He was curious about how soft she might be underneath. When she'd folded herself in half, resting her head on her knees, looking like life had kicked the living daylights out of her, he wanted to pound someone's face to a pulp. He wanted to ease that pain for her. He wanted to solve the problem and bring back her wide, pretty smile. Not that he'd seen it aimed at him. But he'd caught a glimpse at the feed store, and it had nearly knocked his boots off.

Shane sat up, reached behind his head, and tugged off his T-shirt. He'd lost his flannel button-down somewhere in Cricket's living room, having shed it and his boots upon entering the house. He shifted so he was sitting on the side of the bed, then pushed up on his hands and came to a stand. With deft fingers, he undid his jeans and dropped them to his knees before plopping back down on the bedside. He shucked them in two seconds flat. Shane stared at the high tech prosthesis that was now his lower left leg. Admittedly, the carbon fiber foot gave him nearly the same stability and flexibility he'd had with his real foot. The form-fitting socket and vacuum seal over his stump had been perfectly crafted to his shape, making the fit comfortable and as natural as possible.

Considering it *was* replacement parts. The real deal had been comfortable and natural, too. He was still partial to the parts he lost. The originals didn't itch like a son of a bitch like his stump.

Shane broke the seal, sighed with relief, and removed the prosthesis. He rolled the sock down and removed it from his stump. Nope, not one red area to be found. He'd give credit where credit was due; his new leg was impressive. He also had different attachments, one for running and another for swimming, though he'd only used those at rehab. He wasn't ready for folks around here to stare or ask endless questions. Not yet anyway.

Having adjusted to his new one-limb-down status, Shane had worked out the kinks on his bedtime routine. Getting out of bed to do something he'd forgotten, like brush his teeth, was a pain in the ass. Only when he traveled did his routine show flaws. Mostly because he lacked familiarity with the new location. Regardless, he made sure he did all he could before he took the device off or else he'd have to hop around if, like he'd done in the past, left his crutches in another room. He shifted back onto the bed and got comfortable, pillows stacked behind him. He rolled to the side and turned off the bedside lamp, then picked up his phone.

He scrolled through email and clicked on the one that had come earlier while he was at Bryce's with Ellie and everyone. The sender, Captain Tolliver Jones, was Shane's buddy and served in the same command. He scanned the body of the email.

HEY MAN,

How are the cows and horses? I bet you're bored out of your mind. I've been keeping my ears open and pressed to the wall and I heard something interesting today. Looks like there's talk of bringing you in to teach at sniper school. Also talk about you running simulations for training. Guess they figure you got some real time experience. That sounds promising, right? It's not boots on the ground combat but its pretty damn close. Looking forward to you getting your sorry ass back here so I can win some money off you at poker. Your absence is hurting my wallet.

Be cool Devil Dog

TJ

Shane let the phone drop to his side, surprised by the disappointment TJ's email evoked. Logically, he knew the Marines weren't going to let him stay a sniper in the field. Having a bum leg wouldn't be a problem, nor would it stop him from doing what he was trained to do. Until he had to scramble quickly if he found himself in a hot zone. Even then, the move to not put him in the field was more based on "what ifs" instead of fact.

Could he teach? That stupid adage ran through his mind: *those who can do, and those who can't teach.* His lip curled up in disgust. The Gunny Sergeant who taught him was no slacker; he'd put the bad in badass. Shane had enough awarded metal on his uniform shirt to validate his street cred.

But could he do it? And if he did, how long could he do it before he got the itch for something with a little more adrenalin? These were the questions he needed answers to before he made any further decisions. Right now though, he had a long-legged, sexy woman to rescue.

That put a smile on his face, and moments later Shane fell into a heavy sleep. The first one in a long time.

9

WEDNESDAY

Shane arrived at the diner moments after Ellie did. He parked his truck beside hers, then got out and gave it a thorough inspection. Ellie stood by, watching and biting her nails, worried another problem was about to rear its ugly head. When he was done, Shane nodded with satisfaction and took a seat on the bench outside the diner. Spring mornings in Wyoming were lovely, but the air still carried a chill and required a lighter coat. Ellie was happy to be going in the warm diner.

She pushed open the door, then paused and asked. "You're gonna sit there the entire time I'm here?"

"Yeah." He crossed one leg over the other.

He was dressed much like he'd been yesterday. Only today his blue jeans were a dark wash and his flannel shirt was black and red. No jacket. He'd foregone shaving, and the scruff on his jaw gave him a dangerous look. More so than yesterday.

"Why?" She couldn't figure out what he was getting out of this. Maybe he had a knight-in-shining-armor-complex and she was the damsel in distress. Ellie gave a mental shrug, she was definitely in distress.

"If a person were to sit quietly enough and long enough, information can be gathered. When I watch a target I am able to pick up patterns and habits. I can spot weaknesses. Besides, you'd be amazed at what people say when they forget you're around."

Made sense. "Want me to bring you some coffee or something?" Ellie wasn't sure what to say. Pointing out that certain town folk of Wolf Creek would tell anyone anything at any time if they were asked seemed less...boring. She wasn't sure he'd get anything by impersonating a stature. But she didn't want to start out by calling his idea dumb. So she went with Grams steadfast advice--a woman could always get to man through his stomach. Maybe when fed, he'd be ready to hear what she had to say.

"Yeah, sounds good," he grunted as if talking was too laborious.

Clearly not a morning person. "What sounds good, coffee or food?"

"Yeah," he said for the third time. He crossed his arms over his chest.

Ellie shook her head and went inside. She got the coffee going, cut up the potatoes for hash, fried bacon, and made oatmeal. The diner would open in twenty minutes and Ellie, short order cook extraordinaire, had to be ready. Today was Wednesday, and that meant the local vets would be in. After putting together ham, egg, and cheese on an English muffin, she poured coffee into a large mug and took them to Shane. He sat so still she thought he'd fallen asleep or, worse, froze. She stepped in front of him, and his eyes shifted to her. Nothing else about him moved.

"You're creeping me out," she said and placed the mug and food next to him on the bench seat and stepped back.

"You'd be surprised what the brain overlooks when there is no activity." He sat forward so quickly she jumped. "See," he said. "Even though you know I was here, your brain was sending another message."

"Right now my brain's telling me you're odd," she blurt out, pulling open the diner door. She didn't go in.

He surveyed her.

She continued to babble. "I mean, you're sitting right in front. No one is going to mess with my truck if you're *right here*." She pointed to the bench.

"So I've killed two birds with one stone then. I stopped another strike, and I've sent a message to the person." He arched one brow while separating the sandwich from the foil she'd put it in.

"Oh," she said feeling foolish and stupid. "Yeah, I suppose I can see the wisdom in that."

He took a bite of the sandwich and raised it to her in a toast. Then he winked.

Ellie rolled her eyes then went back inside and settled in behind the grill.

After her shift, Shane followed her to the Williamses' ranch and helped her feed the livestock. He also double-checked the premises to make sure the Williams hadn't been targeted as well.

The thought horrified Ellie. If whoever was doing this targeted others to get to her, she wasn't sure what she would do. Imagining it was too terrifying and made her sick to her stomach.

The last stop before going to the farm was the farm stand where Grams worked every morning until noon in the spring and fall and until two in summer. Soon, crops would be coming in, and their hours at the farm stand would increase. Their pocketbooks would be slightly fatter too, but only slightly. Summer was when they made the most. Ellie hadn't had a chance to bring Grams up to speed about Shane and his impending presence on the farm because the older woman had been still asleep when Ellie left for the diner.

The farm stand, situated where the Greenes' driveway intersected the state road, was the size of a small bedroom. The back was the only solid wall, the front and sides were thick vinyl screens that could be rolled up or down depending on the weather. They snapped into place on center and corner beams and were reliable in a strong wind. Ellie's favorite part was the tin roof, weathered from the years of being a community staple.

Ellie parked behind the stand next to Grams's truck, and Shane followed suit. Ellie walked with Shane through the side—Grams had the vinyl rolled up—and greeted Grams who was sitting in a plastic chair, reading.

"How's it going?" Ellie asked while straightening some of the bins.

"On course for a good year, Ellie. Hey there, Shane Hannigan, it's good to see you again. I heard you were just as much a handful over there in them foreign countries as you were in Sunday school." Grams set her book aside, then stood and held open her arms, inviting him in for a hug.

"It's good to see you, too, Mrs. Greene. I tried to be a menace to them, and I apologize for being one to you all those years."

Their exchange reminded Ellie that Shane had a longer history here in Wolf Creek than she did. Grams had probably taught him in Sunday school several years in a row. While she, Ellie, had spent her Sundays in foreign countries slowly making her way here, Shane had spent his years here slowly making his way to foreign countries.

"Either one of you want to tell me what the hell is going on?" Grams settled herself back into her chair behind the register and tapped at her ear. "Damn thing is buzzing again. You'll have to speak up so I can hear you over it."

Ellie went over and adjusted the troublesome hearing aid. "Better?"

"Much," Grams said and patted her hand.

"Listen, Grams, I have something to tell you, and it's not good." Ellie gestured for Shane to pull up the extra plastic chair, and Ellie squatted before her.

Her Grams didn't suffer fools so Ellie felt no need to mince words. "I think someone is targeting us. Causing us trouble. I don't know why. I don't know who. I just know its happening."

Grams looked at Shane. "That's why he's here."

Ellie nodded. "He's offered to help. In fact, Shane was the one who helped me realize these incidents weren't all coincidences."

Shane sat forward and rested his elbows on his knees. "I'd like to help. My folks ranch runs like a well-oiled machine. I'm in limbo. If I can be of help to you all, that would be great." Shane put up a hand. "I know you both are more than capable. I'm not saying you aren't. I'm saying a fresh set of eyes might be good."

Grams flexed her biceps and pointed to hers then to Shane's. "And some guns like the size of yours won't hurt either."

Shane laughed. "There is that. If whoever is targeting you has hired someone, then having a guy around might dissuade him."

Grams shrugged. "Let's hope."

Shane cleared his throat. "If it's no trouble, I'd like you both to make a list of all the issues you've had on the farm. And a list of people who you think might be responsible. Think outside the box. Fort said the likelihood that this is someone we all know is close to one-hundred percent."

Grams brows rose slightly. "That's not a good feeling."

"No, it's not." Ellie shook her head. "To think someone who knows us set up the gate so any of the goats could get hurt. This person has probably been around our goats, and they still did it. That's disturbing."

A moment of silence hung between them, each considering the ramifications of such an accusation.

Ellie slapped her thighs, then stood. "If you're good to hang here a while longer, I'll take Shane back to the farm and let him inspect. He and Bryce are going to try and hunt this coyote this evening, too." Typically, Ellie would relieve Grams so she could go home and rest.

Grams waved Ellie off. "Of course, I'm good to sit here. I'm old, not decrepit." She chuckled. "There's only a few hours left anyways."

"I'll come back then and help you load the truck with what's left," Ellie said and gestured for Shane to follow her.

"Be mindful of who comes by and offers to help," Shane cautioned Grams.

She replied with another breezy wave.

At the farm, Ellie led Shane through the barn and out the back door. The goats were in the yard. She pointed to the large Saanen goats with their white coats and large flat ears. He'd gotten out of his truck with binoculars round his neck and a shotgun in his hand. A mixture of relief and anxiety trembled through her. He would be a tremendous help, but at what cost? Would she become dependent on someone else to solve her problems and fix the farm?

"We started out with two Saanen. It was Grams idea. I'm lactose intolerant, and she thought having goats to milk would provide me with dairy and might be another income source for us. Turns out, she was right." Ellie scanned the yard and pointed to the far corner. "Total Saanen count is at ten now."

Shane leaned across a fence and pointed to a Nigerian Dwarf running by. Both her front legs were cast and her gait was part hobble part hop. "What's going on here?"

"Watch," Ellie said and pointed to another Nigerian Dwarf with a black and white coat. "That's Run Around Sue. We call her 'ninja goat.' Her front right hoof has a prosthesis. She was trampled by some cows when she was a baby. That happens more than people realize. Sue lost her front hoof and has damage to her right eye. She's partially blind, but that doesn't stop her from trying to own the yard."

Sue ran up a ramp in the yard, sprung off the end, and catapulted over a large Saanen goat. She hit the ground running, ran in a circle three times, then ran up to another goat and jumped over her, leaping from her back.

Shane laughed. "She has lots of energy."

"That's an understatement. She goes non-stop. The goat she jumped over is Lucy. Benny the Jet is her favorite to terrorize. He'll chase her all day long."

Shane squatted to look at Lucy. "I see a theme here with your pet names. Lucy has a diamond on her forehead so let me take a stab at this. 'Lucy in the Sky with Diamonds?'"

Ellie smiled and nodded. "They practically name themselves."

Shane walked around the yard and stopped outside the pen. "Who built this?" He ran his hand down the structure.

"I did. I also built the obstacle course for them." Ellie pointed to the playground of ramps, stairs, and platforms in various heights the goats were running up and down.

"You've got skill. These cuts are really well done." He tapped his finger to the mitered corners.

"My grandfather had good tools, so I put them to use. I suppose my parents being missionaries and me being forced into that lifestyle paid off." She shrugged. "A person can learn a lot in a third-world country. My biggest regret was not learning mechanical things." She pointed to an old, slightly rusted, lateral pivot irrigation system that was up against the barn. The system, a series of overhead sprinklers that rolled through the crops, was an efficient way to manage irrigation. When it worked. "That's been out of commission for two months."

Shane looked over at the crops. "How you watering?"

Ellie laughed. "Old-school hoses with holes in them. Ground sprinklers. More labor involved but running our farm stand is too important to lose. I was hoping to start a CSA for the fall, but I can't manage the crops with hoses."

"What's all that?" Shane pointed to the pasture beyond the crops. "Didn't that used to be more crops?"

Ellie nodded. "It did. But we couldn't keep it up with the irrigation system down. We had a hired hand, but we had to let him go when we lost those crops. My goal was to try and get it tilled again for fall crops."

"Who all knew that?" Shane glanced to Ellie then back to the field. He shaded his eyes with his hand.

Ellie gave a half shrug. "I suppose Mr. Landry and Mr. Phillips. We might have mentioned it to them. Also my mom. I probably told her one time when she called. We don't have a lot to talk about. I'm not sure who all Grams told."

"What about the field beyond?" The terrain looked rockier, more scrub brush and less grass that eventually became part of the foothills. "Is that part of the property?"

"Yeah, and one time Gramps found a large sapphire out there. Those foothills have all kinds of minerals and gemstones." Ellie chuckled sardonically. "Maybe I should just spend my time out there looking for another sapphire. That would sure come in handy."

Shane faced her. "Have you tried?"

Ellie rolled her eyes. "And waste my time? That would be like looking for a needle in a haystack. No, one needle in a four-wide haystack. No thanks. Gramps only found his out of sheer luck."

"Some women would spend endless hours seeking a giant gem," Shane teased.

Ellie pointed her thumbs at her chest. "Not this one. If I had a good rock, I'd hock it for cash and give Grams peace of mind."

Shane studied her. Under his gaze, Ellie was uncomfortable. The first time they'd seen each other, he'd studied her in the way a man checks out a woman. Now, his expression was curious, puzzled even. Ellie smiled smugly. Men always underestimated her. Maybe it was because she didn't talk a lot or because she liked to stick to herself. Honestly though, Ellie had long stopped caring why they underestimated her. She didn't have anything to prove.

And yet, his approval and admiration of her work had been oddly rewarding. She met his gaze with her own and sparks arced between them. Magnetic tendrils wrapped around them, the force pushing them closer. Whenever he stood near her, her body became inconveniently heated.

Ellie considered his broad shoulders and large hands and instantly had naughty thoughts about her hands gripping his shoulders as he ran his hands all over her body. Ellie shivered. His touch was something she curiously wanted to experience, yet desperately needed to avoid.

Shane Hannigan was trouble. He wasn't obtainable. He was the sort that needed a thrill, or life would become boring and monotonous. Men like Shane never really entered into anything. They always had one foot out the door.

Shane cleared his throat and shifted away. "Show me the gate."

Ellie ducked her head so he wouldn't see her swallow. Afraid he'd read her desire. "Er, ah, it's this way." She led him through the yard toward the gate.

They stood on the inside of the yard while Shane messed with the gate, dropping to one knee to check the mechanism.

"Yeah, it was forcibly broken. Look here." He turned to her and gestured for her to come down to his level. "If you look from underneath, you can see the scratches."

Ellie knelt down, her head close to his shoulder as she followed the angle of his arm up to the area he was pointing. Sure enough, the lock had been lifted up and away from the gate so it wouldn't line up with the catching mechanism.

Ellie continued to squat, her hands on her knees. "I think the weather that evening, the storm coming in, kept blowing the gate open, and that's how the goats got out." Yes, the lock was broken, but the gate hadn't been set open to let the goats out. Had it?

Shane rocked back on his heels and grunted his doubt. A wisp of a grimace crossed his face. "Look around, Ellie. You really think the wind blew it open and a coyote just happened to be in the neighborhood? Before twilight? Doesn't add up."

She shrugged, not wanting to entertain the scary thoughts.

When she scanned the yard, something in the distance caught her eye. "What's that?"

Shane lifted the binoculars, grunted again, and then stood. She stood, too.

"It looks like a dead rabbit." He removed the binoculars from around his neck and handed them to her. "Look about twenty yards past it. There's another one."

He was right.

"Someone baited the area?" It was an old hunter's trick to use road kill and other dead animals to bait out coyotes.

Shane pointed to a small mound of dirt on the other side of the gate. It looks to have been higher but the previous night's rain had reduced it. "Likely used to keep the gate open. Whoever did this knew a storm was coming and knew it would wash away the dirt. I think its more likely the wind was strong enough to blow the gate closed, which is how you saw it."

Ellie put her head in her hands and drew in a deep, ragged breath. "Oh, god."

Shane touched her shoulder. "Hey, it's okay. We'll fix this." He stepped closer and squeezed both her shoulders between his hands as if infusing strength into her.

She looked into his sexy deep brown eyes, not ashamed of the tears threatening to break free from hers. "I can't let Grams down."

"We won't. I promise. Hey, don't cry." Using the side of his index finger, he lifted away the tear.

There was a basic connection between them she felt it deep in her soul. She couldn't explain it because it was a new experience. The feeling reminded her of kinship since last time she'd felt this connected to anyone was Grams. She could, however, be mistaking this deep bond for kindness, something she rarely allowed herself to accept. Or maybe it was because she hadn't been sexually attracted to anyone in, oh say, forever. Shane was sex on a stick. A dead woman would rise from her grave for his attention. Ellie's gaze fell to his mouth and his wide, soft lips. They were meant for kissing.

Without a second thought, Ellie gave into impulse, rose onto her toes, and planted her lips on his. She pressed slightly before easing herself away. She liked the contrast of his smooth lips to the scruff of his beard.

His brow furrowed. He asked quizzically, "What was that?"

Ellie reared back slightly. "That was a kiss."

"Um, no, it wasn't." He gave a small shake of his head. "That was a peck, like what a chicken does. Or maybe a push like what your goats do when they butt their head into you. But it was definitely not a kiss. You need to spend a little less time with animals and a lot more with people."

Ellie took a step back in shock. Heat blossomed over her chest, and any moment now it would rise up to stain her entire face the color of a strawberry.

"I, um..." The words caught in her throat so all she managed was, "Gak."

Then she did the only thing she knew to do. She spun on her heel and speed-walked away. Because running, after all, would be even more embarrassing.

10

WEDNESDAY

"W here you going?" Shane called to her retreating back, smirking as he watched her beat feet away. He'd thrown her for a loop.

She waved a hand in the air, but he had no clue what that meant. "I'll just walk the perimeter then, see how long the bait trail is."

She waved again.

Shane chuckled. Getting under her skin gave him pleasure. Not because he liked to rile people, though he did for some, but because she'd seemed unflappable. She'd stood in front of her second flat tire in as many days and told him she didn't need his help.

He'd done it. He'd penetrated her armor, and underneath her heavy shield, he'd seen a wanton beauty. For the first time in years, Shane's focus was on something other than his job. He was consumed with the curly-haired cutie.

Swinging his shotgun over his shoulder, he pushed through the gate and out into what Ellie called the outer yard, what he would call a pasture. The rivets in the ground from the previous crops made walking the land more difficult with his prosthesis. He was less sure-footed, just like her disabled goats would be, making it hard for them to escape a predator.

Like all farmers, the Greenes had to rotate their crops in order to not tax the soil. Currently, the land wasn't being used for anything other than grazing and a bait trail for coyotes. Shane followed the trail away from the animals and toward the tree line that would lead to the forest.

He lifted the binoculars and scanned the ground. Chances were the coyotes had eaten everything up to this point and left the rabbits behind when they spotted Benny, a live, fresh goat.

"Dolly," Ellie called, her tone an octave higher than normal. She then gave a sharp whistle. "What are you messing with?" Shane swung around, spotted Dolly the llama near the far side of the barn, and pointed the binoculars in the direction of what she was tentatively poking at, jumping back after every poke.

Shane swore under his breath. Looked to be a rattler, a fat one at that. The snake was coiled, primed to strike, whipping its tail rapidly in warning.

In one fluid motion, Shane released the binoculars while pulling his rifle forward and sighting it. The binoculars bounced against his chest when the strap caught, but Shane barely processed it, singularly focused on the snake.

"Ellie, stay back," he called when he caught sight of her moving toward the llama in his periphery.

"What is it?" she called back.

Shane waited a beat, knowing he was on borrowed time, but didn't want to catch Dolly leaning forward. He saw a pattern in her pokes, three seconds between the llama pulling back before poking again. He sighted, counted the pattern in his head, and just as Dolly recoiled, Shane exhaled and pulled the trigger all at once. Both Dolly and the snake jumped, the snake from the impact of the bullet, and Dolly ran off toward the barn. Shane was confident the snake hadn't struck before he got off his shot, but he needed to see the animal to be sure. He jogged to the snake, Ellie to the llama. He wished his prosthesis was able to morph into what he needed when he needed because his running leg would make this endeavor easier.

Ellie reached Dolly first and was inspecting her face. "I don't think she was bit. I'm bringing her into the yard."

Shane considered the dead snake. A prairie rattlesnake. Not totally uncommon in these areas but more common east of the continental divide. Wolf Creek was decidedly *not* east of the Continental Divide.

Shane scanned the area and found a depression in the grass that could be a footstep. He moved in closer to inspect. Because of the rain the previous night, the mark was clear enough. It was definitely a boot imprint. The tread markings indicated a type of waterproof boot. And whoever had left these had done so after the rains had passed.

"Ellie, does your grandmother come out here, and does she wear waterproof boots?" He didn't want to jump to assumptions. He looked beyond the displaced dirt for more imprints and saw another downward depression in a patch of dry grass.

"She typically doesn't do either. Her hip's been bothering her so she's overly cautious about falling." Ellie was moving toward him, now in the enclosure with the goats and Dolly.

Shane tracked the depressions, walking parallel to the enclosed yard. Ellie followed, the fence between them.

Sure enough, there was a path of footsteps. From where he stood, they looked to round the far side of the barn, the side out of view from the farmhouse. The impressions were more embedded in the earth where the footprints started.

As if the person was carrying something heavy when they arrived.

Every few steps there looked to be the impression of a ring. Large and round. *A bucket.*

Shane turned around and faced the path he'd followed. He wanted an estimate of the person's height, and he could do that by measuring the stride to his own. Without looking over his shoulder, Shane took a step back, using his mental measurements of the previous footsteps. His footstep lined up perfectly with the ones on the ground. It was a broad assumption, but Shane felt a shorter person couldn't have made the long strides. A tall person like himself, over six feet likely, left the footprints.

And the snake.

Yep, the impressions were definitely deeper as he followed the path away from the dead snake. No doubt about it, the person had been carrying something, and it had started out heavy.

Shane took another step backward. He saw a deeper imprint.

"You think someone planted that snake?" Ellie's voice was hushed.

His gaze darted to hers. "Yep." He glanced back at the ground and tried to piece a timeline of events together, wondering about when they snake had been dropped off. Could have been as recent as this morning. The ground was still wet.

Shane took another step backward, one more in line with the far corner of the barn. From here he couldn't see the house. Anyone in the house couldn't see him. If he shifted to his left, he would be alongside the barn and Ellie, stuck behind the fence, would be out of sight as well.

Shane put his right foot back, his left already in motion to follow when he heard the unmistakable sound of a snake's tail rattling. He eased the tip of his boot toe to touch the ground trying to balance himself. When Shane swayed, his gaze darted to Ellie's.

She gasped and leaned over the fence the best she could, her focus on the area around his feet. "To your left. Its mouth is agape." Meaning, the snake was getting into strike position.

Shane nodded and began to slowly lower his foot inch by inch until his boot heel connected with a large rock.

The rattling increased.

The combination of the uneven surface and Shane's limited

flexibility with the prosthetic foot forced him to rock to his right side. Shane shifted forward, trying to balance without throwing up his arms and startling the snake. He was seconds too late, too unfamiliar with his new leg and how to adjust. A moment like this was what his rehab doc would call a "teachable one." Shane would have preferred there not be a real rattler while he learned it. He continued to teeter forward and away from the snake, forcing his left leg to come up and punch out toward the snake.

He was going over. He knew he wouldn't be able to get a shot off in time. His angle was all wrong. He had a one second to make a decision.

He caught Ellie's eye. "Catch," he said and tossed the rifle.

In the same second he went down, she caught the rifle and sighted it on the snake.

Unfortunately, timing wasn't on their side as the snake struck out, sinking its fangs into Shane's pant leg. When it reared back to go at Shane a second time, Ellie blasted three shots into the snake. Head, body, and body. Because it was a super long body. The last two were for good measure and because she was scared witless.

"Shane," she screamed. She tossed the rifle over the fence and, using the side of the barn and the post, vaulted herself over the side.

Shane sat up on his elbows and looked at the snake. Falling had jarred his injured hip, and pain was shooting up and down his side. He nodded to the snake. "Wow, nice shot." Then he fell back and let his hands drop to his side. He closed his eyes, needing a moment to catch his breath.

Ellie slid to a stop by his head, spraying dirt around him. She cupped his face between her hands. "Are you okay? Look at me."

Following a grunt, Shane opened his eyes while pushing her hands from his face. "I'm okay."

Ellie ran her hands down his body, patting his chest and then his hips. "Anything broken? Don't panic. Try to keep your heartrate steady. Did he only get you in the leg?" She continued to pat him, working down to his thighs. She paused long enough to kick the snake away, the body still twitching and the rattle still shaking.

"I'm going to take a look at the bite," she said, reaching for his bottom pant cuff.

Shane sat up quickly, ignoring the sharp pain in his hip, and pushed her hands away. "I'm fine."

"We have to know if you were bit." She slapped his hands and went for his pant leg.

"Ellie, the snake bit my boot. I didn't get bit. Just the wind knocked out of me. Stop." He pushed her hands away again. Much like the foot-fight he and Cricket engaged in, Shane and Ellie engaged in a scuffle of the hands, one set trying to stop the other.

"Ellie, dammit," Shane roared, "stop."

Her hands stilled, her brow narrowed, and she said tartly, "I'm only trying to make sure you're okay."

"I said I was."

"Yes, but men say that all the time and don't mean it."

She had him there. The entire time he was being medevac'd to the naval hospital, he'd complained about being removed from the field, insisting he was more than capable to return to duty. Even with a portion of his leg missing.

"I need to see to be sure. I won't have peace of mind until." Ellie crossed her arms over her chest.

"The snake bit my boot." He pulled his pant leg up to show her the upper quarter of the boot where it zipped, making sure to keep the prosthesis covered. "See?" He nodded to the marks on his boot. He was glad he'd worn his Danner Pronghorn's since they were specifically designed to withstand a snakebite. But that's not what had driven Shane to select the boots. They were lighter than his cowboy boots and the fit was adjustable allowing him to make them tighter thereby giving him more support.

Fat lot of good that did him as he was twisting and falling to the ground.

"Show me where your leg didn't get punctured or scraped," she challenged.

He tucked his hand over the rim to feel the inside of the boot, staring at her hard so she wouldn't look away. "Ellie, I can feel through the boots that the fangs didn't go all the way through. My leg doesn't hurt at all. He pulled out his hand and wagged his fingers. "No blood." He didn't like deceiving her.

She inspected his hand. "You swear you weren't bit?"

He crossed his heart.

She let out a breath in a loud whoosh of air and flopped down beside him, opposite side of the snake, of course. "Jeez, that scared me." She lay on her back, arm thrown over her eyes. "What if you had been bit. What if Grams had been bit. Or anyone." She glanced at him from under her arm. "You know when the last time I saw a rattler on our property?"

Shane shook his head.

"Never, and I've been here for twelve years. Now there's two?" She covered her eyes again. "This is getting serious."

Shane chuckled. "Sweetheart, it's been serious. You're just now accepting that?"

"You're right," she mumbled.

"Where did you learn to shoot like that? I'm impressed." He rested up on one elbow, turned on his good side, and stared down at her.

"Remember those missionary parents I mentioned?"

Shane grunted his affirmation.

"When living in Africa, its smart for all people to learn how to survive. I was an astute learner, particularly for shelter and protection. Finding food was right up there, too. I learned to get creative with what we had and to look around the environs for what I could use. I also learned to do it myself and not wait for help."

"Did you like living out there?" She intrigued him. This

woman with the hair so curly it bounced and sprang around her head when she walked.

"Nope," she said without hesitation. "For most of it, I was a kid. I wanted to be somewhere with a mall and a movie theater. I resented living out there. When I finally convinced my parents to let me stay here for high school I thought I'd won the lottery." She grinned sheepishly. "Don't get me wrong. I like helping people. I like bringing comfort to people."

"But?" He picked up a curly lock and pulled it out, then let it go to spring back in place. He related to the bobbing curl. He felt like he was bungee-ing through life, too.

"But, and this makes me terrible person, it felt like living hard would never end. We would never have running water, much less a private bath. And I was tired of always being dirty or slightly hungry or vigilant."

"That doesn't make you a terrible person. That makes you human." He brushed a knuckle over her cheek, swiping away a streak of dirt.

Ellie sighed. "Except both my parents are still there. Have been there for years. They don't seem to mind the hardship of that life. All it took was for Brad to suggest we get married and spend our lives doing what my folks were doing for me to get the heck out of there." She lifted her arm from her eyes. "When the guy you've been dating for two years says he'd like to marry you, a girl is typically excited, right?"

Shane shrugged one shoulder. "I wouldn't know, but I'll take your word for it. Continue. I have a feeling this is going to be a great story."

Ellie rolled her eyes.

"What did you do when the fabulous Brad hinted about marriage?"

"I split. We had an airport run scheduled for that night, a supply pickup. I left everything behind including a note to my parents that I needed to try college. I got on the first plane out of there and came to Grams."

"So after high school you left here and went back to Africa?" Shane found her life captivating. Almost similar to his, sort of.

"They were in Bangladesh when I came to live here for high school. Then after graduation they were in South Sudan. I was there almost two years."

"Hard countries. So you ditched Brad with a Dear John letter, came back here, and went to college?" He'd stopped brushing the dirt from her cheek and was now lightly pushing her hair from her face, his thumb caressing her forehead and temple as he did so.

"Sorta. I tried college, but I didn't like it." She glanced away, looking toward the farmhouse.

"Dropped out?" he asked curiously.

"More like just stopped going. Packed my bags and left."

Shane arched his brows. He'd pick up on the fact she liked to split when life wasn't going her way. "What did you study?"

"Nursing at first. Like my mom, but I have no interest. And then teaching. My parents thought either of those would be good skills to have as a missionary, and after having bolted without saying goodbye, I kinda thought I owed it to them to try. They kept saying if I had a trade or skill, I'd like living there better." She shook her head. "I'm fairly confident nothing could make me like it there better. I like here better. I like here best of all."

"You seem to have found your niche here." He loved how smooth her skin was. How, as she talked about herself, her cheeks colored ever so slightly. Ellie was the type of girl he liked, the kind that didn't like to go on and on about herself.

"Maybe," she whispered.

Their eyes met and held and once again, the attraction between them palpable. Shane could cup it in his hand, but knew the charge would shock him. He could feel the energy humming through his body.

"Remember that kiss you gave me?" he asked, his voice husky.

Ellie shut her eyes and groaned. "Do we have to talk about it?"

"Only because I'm going to show you what a real kiss is like. Hold on to your boots, Ellie Greene, I'm about to blow them off."

Ellie's eyes sprang open. Then she laughed, a reaction he wasn't expecting. She snorted. "I can't wait. I've heard these sorts of promises before. Have yet to lose my boots."

Shane, resting on his forearms, cupped her face between his hands and lowered himself so he hovered barely above her, his chest touching hers. He brushed his lips softly across hers. Once, twice, and on the third, he stayed, holding the kiss. He teased her lips open and slid his tongue into her mouth, tasting her fully. When she touched her tongue to his, he sucked hers into his mouth gently. When Ellie groaned, he deepened the kiss, explored her more openly, inviting her to join him.

She met his kiss with all the vigor she was keeping bridled. When she wrapped her arms around his neck, Shane scooped her up, sliding his arms beneath her. The fervor of their kiss increased before they broke apart briefly to gasp in air and return for more. He rolled them so she was on top of him. He ran his hands up her legs then waist, bringing them to rest over her breasts.

Ellie moaned and tossed back her head. Shane tugged her shirt from her jeans waistband, desperately needing to touch her skin. He slipped his hand beneath her shirt, the tips of his fingers brushing against her stomach as he traveled them upward. Eager to be closer, to feel more of her against him, he sat up effectively placing her in his lap. Through the sheer cloth of her bra, he rolled her nipple between his thumb and index finger. She kissed him with the hunger of a starving woman, occasionally nipping at his chin. He had one hand on the small of her back, pushing her into him hard, grinding.

"Let's get naked," he whispered then trailed hot kisses down her neck.

Ellie jumped and squared up as if the snake had bitten her. Her hands came to her cheeks, not even remotely covering the flush that was spreading up her throat to her face. "Oh, my word. What are we doing? I don't even know you." She sounded shocked.

"But it's good, right? You were having a good time. I, in case you were wondering, was having a helluva good time. I want to have some more." He reached for her.

She slapped at his hands. "I don't do things like this."

Shane let his hands fall to his side. "Things like what? Enjoy yourself?"

"Yeah," she said and stood. She gasped and looked at her feet. Her boots were missing.

Shane chuckled and pointed behind her where her boots lay.

"What? How? Oh, never mind!" She scurried toward them, grabbing them up as she passed.

"Hey, where you going?" he called after her.

"I...ah... I..." She looked over her shoulder and picked up speed.

"You can't run away, Ellie. I'm still going to be here," Shane called out. "Besides, you live here." He chuckled and rolled to his side, pushing up. "I'm not going away."

She was a blur in the wind, making it to the house before he had his pants dusted off and his hard-on under control. As if he could ever have his hard-on fully under control around this woman.

The fire burning deep inside her was just begging to be set free, and Shane was feeling like an arsonist.

11

SATURDAY

S hane spent the last few days following the snakebite scare hanging out with Ellie, much to her dismay. He went everywhere she did. Often, he'd find her staring at his lips or his chest. Once even his groin. He'd had to turn away then because the heat from her gaze had caused a woody, and she wasn't ready to take that on.

Ellie was skittish as a filly. He hadn't fully figured her out yet. He did know she wasn't used to attention of any sort, particularly sexual interest. And he had that for her in abundance. All he had to do to get her flustered was wink at her or lean against the hay bales and watch her while she cooed over and loved on her goats.

Shane liked this for two reasons. One, it had been a long time since he'd flirted with a pretty girl. Especially one who was as interested as he was. Two, their playful banter and her tendency to overthink everything kept her mind of the scary stuff. Just yesterday he'd found a device stuck in her tire. It was a pin-like object used to deflate tires over time. Whoever was doing this wasn't put off by Shane's presence. Or knew at least to come at night when Shane was gone.

Yesterday, Shane had ridden the Greenes' property and fixed two fallen fence posts and a section of fencing where the wires had been cut. After showing Ellie the cuts, her anxiety had increased. Only bringing her little goat Benny home had taken her mind off the farm's issues. Right now, Ellie had the goat cradled to her in some sort of baby sling thing while she cleaned out stalls, fed animals, and chatted up a storm with them.

She was cooing to Benny, rubbing his head when she went into the empty stall where the Greenes stored the hay and grain for feed. Shane followed her in. When she turned around, he smiled down at her and reached out, petting Benny. He took a step toward her; she took a step back. They did this slow dance until her back was up against the stall wall.

"Are you trying to scare me?" She'd placed her hands on her hips, but the quiver in her voice gave away her jitteriness.

"Nope," he said, still petting Benny, "just trying to get your attention."

Ellie did a half-chuckle snort. "Oh, well. You've got it." Her cheeks turned pink.

"My folks want me to come over for dinner."

She hitched her lip up in confusion. "Okay, have fun."

"They invited you and your grandmother."

"Tonight?" She gulped.

"Yeah, sorry for the late notice. My mom cornered me this morning at Cricket's and wouldn't let me leave until I promised to invite you. You can bring your little baby here, if you want." He stroked Benny's head.

"So, this is your mom asking. Not you. If you had a choice, you'd not have me come?" she challenged.

"If I had my choice, we'd do some of this." He pushed her against the wall, careful not to squeeze the little special needs goat, his hands on Ellie's shoulders, his hips lined up with hers. He swooped down and delivered a firm kiss. The minute his lips touched hers, she owned him. He would do anything she asked. If only she knew. Shane had spent years giving all his love to the Marine Corp. What he was experiencing with Ellie was refreshing. Maybe, if he did end up taking that job as an instructor, he would consider a relationship. He wouldn't be deployed anymore. He'd be around to actually fulfill his role as a partner.

He swept kisses across her cheeks, chin, and back to her lips. He teased her with his tongue, inviting hers to come out and play. The heat of passion and sexual need rose between then, and Shane was consumed with the desire to strip off all his and Ellie's clothes.

He gripped her hips and rhythmically rubbed against her, mindful of the little goat in the sling between them.

"Dammit, you're sexy," he groaned and worked kisses down the column of her neck.

Ellie moaned and little Benny bleated. Shane froze. Benny bleated again louder. Shane rocked back on his heels to consider the goat. The fawn-colored animal looked directly at him and bleated so loud Shane took a step back, as if he was being yelled at. Cockblocked by a tiny goat in a sling.

"I think he doesn't like being this up close to the action," Ellie said. She sagged against the wall.

"Maybe not bring him tonight." Shane held his hands out to his side. "It's every man for himself."

Ellie laughed. "I get the impression from you that a healthy competition is something you enjoy."

"Are you saying my competition is a goat?" Shane spread his legs wide to take the weight off his prosthesis and crossed his arms over his chest. He also moved to block her from dashing away as she liked to do.

"Are you saying you even want competition? I thought you were here to help me figure out who's trying to destroy my farm?" She narrowed her eyes at him. He knew the wheels were working in her brain, trying to find a reason for his desire for her, believing it disingenuous.

"You're considering me again as the culprit, aren't you? Think I concocted all this to get into your pants. I didn't. Go through the timeline again. I wasn't even here. I didn't even know you until earlier this week. I'm here to help, but if we can have a little fun while we get to the bottom of this, then where's the harm in that?"

"Said the wolf to the chicken." She gave him a pointed look and then cut her eyes to the exit behind him. She stood taller against the wall.

She was probably calculating her escape. He wasn't going to let her have it this time.

"Well, stop being such a chicken. You work your butt off. You should have a little fun." He cut her off before she could begin a protest. "Fun outside of mothering your goats. You're like that martyr single mom who does everything for her kids and nothing for herself." Shane chuckled. "Hey, did you like my joke. Get it? Goats, kids. Baby goats are kids—"

She waved off his joke with a dismissive hand. Angrily she said, "I get it. I don't like being called a martyr. I have fun."

"Doing what?" He rocked on his heels and nearly lost his balance, catching himself in time.

"I sew, make goat milk products, I'm developing our CSA." She nodded as if to say "so there."

"Everything you said is work. You sell those products." He shook his head. "Try again."

"I enjoy doing them. I love my work—"

He interrupted in a singsong voice, "But that's not having fun."

"I think its fun."

"Fun with other people. Fun for the sake of doing nothing. Just letting yourself go and enjoying the moment. Look at you. If I step one foot to the right, you'd dash out of her so fast little Benny would get motion sickness. You can't even have a conversation about pleasure."

She groaned. Her eyes darted from the door to the floor.

Busted, and she knew it.

83

Shane continued, "We'll start with a little fun tonight. Dinner at my parents. Of course, it'll be more fun for you than me as you'll get to watch me being tortured. But if you don't find that titillating enough, I can think of stuff we can do afterward you might like." He reached out and tweaked the hard nipple of her right breast. It had been pressing against her thin T-shirt, begging him to touch it. He guessed the other nipple was just as excited, but the sling covered it. Sadly.

Ellie gasped and slapped at his hand. "Oh, my word. You did not just—"

"Yep, and you liked it." He wanted to do it again. Hell, he wanted to kiss her until the heat they created singed that T-shirt right off her body.

"You're a Neanderthal!" she said and brushed at her breast, making the bud harder.

"Yep." There was no denying his caveman tendencies, or his instant woody. "I'll pick you up at five. Text me and let me know if Grams is coming, and I'll bring a more comfortable ride." He stepped aside and gestured with his hand that she was free to go.

She hesitated, the conflicting emotions clearly expressed on her face. She didn't want to run away, but the urge was too strong. He almost felt bad for putting her in the position, but she'd held her own longer than any other confrontation they'd had, and he was proud of that.

Giving in to her need to escape, she scuttled by him without making eye contact. Shane softly bawked like a chicken.

"Shut up," she yelled over her shoulder.

FIVE O'CLOCK on the nose Shane pulled up to the house. Ellie hadn't known what to wear and went with Grams suggestion of a knee length denim skirt, tall brown knee-high boots, and a Paisley western shirt with a tank top underneath. Casual but not daily farm-working clothes. Grams, feigning a headache, had elected to stay home. She let her hair fall in a billion corkscrew curls around her face. She'd thought about texting Shane several times and canceling but knew he'd never except that. He'd likely come to collect her and throw her over his shoulder like some throwback chest-beater.

The thought of it made her knees weak. Not because she liked Neanderthals, but because there was something about the attention he showed her. Maybe it was that he cared enough to come collect her? No one had ever cared that much, and how pathetic was that? On a scale of one to ten with one being not caring and ten being love and adoration, Shane's attention was probably in the six zone. The people, Grams aside, who were supposed to love her would fall below Shane's six Case in point, the day following her escape from Africa had ended before anyone noticed she'd left. She'd been sitting on her Grams's couch sipping tea, confessing her fears, when her mother had called and asked if Grams knew anything. They'd only just discovered her absence and letter.

Stuff like that could really jack up a girl's self-esteem.

Shane held the truck door open for her. "You are gorgeous. You know that, right? I love this crazy hair of yours." He leaned in really close.

Ellie, the seatbelt in her hand and halfway across her chest, froze and forgot how to breathe. His gaze was eating her up, and she felt flames of lust lick at her skin. Jeepers, this man!

"Want me to kiss you?" he whispered. His eyes were on her lips, one hand brushing back the curls from her cheek.

"I, ah… It's not really flattering to say my hair is crazy." It was all she could think of to say because anything else would be a "yes" or "please" or "kiss me now."

Shane caressed her cheek then moved out of her space, closing the door softly.

Ellie sucked in a ragged breath. How was she going to make it through dinner?

The Hannigan ranch was everything a ranch was supposed to be. The fences were intact and in good condition, the animals, beef and dairy cows, were tagged with high-tech tracking and branding, and ranch help was everywhere. They were what made the Hannigan ranch a business and not some crappy start-up piecemeal operation like she and Grams had.

Ellie sighed wistfully. Once upon a time, the farm had been a player in providing local produce. Now it seemed every year a finger slipped on the tedious hold they had on viable money-making jobs.

The Hannigan's moderately-sized rambler style home was painted light gray and stood out clean and fresh against the bright green manicured lawn and blooming annuals. Behind it sat the traditional red barn with a bright blue steel roof. The ambiance was inviting and Shane's parents overly welcoming.

Mrs. Hannigan folded her into a hug. "I'm so sorry you're having troubles, but I'm relieved that you have Shane helping you. Cricket told me what happened to your little goat, and I was horrified."

Mrs. Hannigan was an older version of Cricket. Fair coloring and honey-brown hair.

"Thankfully, Benny's recovering well." Ellie blushed from the attention.

"Its hard enough when nature interferes with our animals, but a deliberate act." She shook her head. "I hope you catch them and press charges, even knowing it's probably someone I call friend. That makes me even angrier." She briefly squeezed Ellie's upper arm in sympathy.

"Don't get her started, please. She's been on a rant since Shane told her what was going on." Shawn Hannigan extended his hand to shake. He was whom Shane got his looks from. Both men had darker complexion and hair, though Mr. Hannigan's was graying. He bore the skin of a man who lived his life out of doors, and the calluses on his hand told of the hard work he did.

The Hannigan parents led her into a large family room-kitchen open concept. A fire warmed the large space. Even though spring was right around the corner, a setting sun brought in cooler night temperatures.

Family pictures lined the wall. The variety of school shots and candids showed a family over the years. Laughter, accomplishments, holidays, were all captured. Ellie's heart contracted with a longing so deep and profound she almost staggered as she passed. A hallway like this was something she'd always wanted. It spoke of consistency and commitment. For years she'd stuffed that need deep down inside her, denying it existed. Because what person wishes their parents wouldn't have wanted to help others or had done so from their home? What person wishes they would've had a typical life of riding a bus to school and growing up with the same people? Of having roots? Sadly, Ellie did not have the same spirit her parents did. Learning with the jungle or African plains as her backdrop hadn't been cool or amazing. Her existence had been isolating. Plagued by a shyness she'd fought years to overcome, Ellie had not made friends easily and sometimes not at all.

What she would have given to have what Shane and his sisters did. Ellie was well aware that her life had been a dream, and someone somewhere would have given anything for what she had. That didn't stop her from wishing it had been different.

"Ellie?"

Ellie's reverie was broken. She turned to Shane's mother who had clearly asked her a question based on her expectant expression.

"I'm sorry. I was busy admiring the pictures on the wall." Ellie took a seat on the couch. Shane sat next to her.

"Sometimes, I stop and get lost in all the memories." Mrs. Hannigan put her hand to heart, briefly forlorn in her own remembrance. She shook her head. "I asked if you'd heard from your parents? You father went to high school with Shawn."

Ellie shook her head. "Not often. They're busy."

"And do they know about what's going on?" Dottie Hannigan asked.

"You mean with the accidents?"

Shane grunted in displeasure.

Ellie quickly said, "I mean incidents."

"Call them what they are. Accidents mean they weren't deliberate, and do you really think someone broke the gate lock hoping none of the animals would get hurt? Particularly your little goats?" Shane's questions were gentle.

Ellie shook her head again, her lips pressed tightly together. Thinking about sweet Benny's injury was still too painful for her. The wound was still too tender for him to wear a harness. She could tell he missed his jet, missed getting around on his own.

"I hope you figure out who is doing it soon. It worries me with you and Minnie out there alone," Mrs. Hannigan said.

"We have Shane most of the time," Ellie reminded her and went to pat Shane's knee. He jumped and took her hand, squeezing it in his and keeping their palms clasped.

"And for that I'm thankful." Mrs. Hannigan waved a dismissive hand toward Shane and said to Ellie, "I know he's got one foot out the door. I know he can't wait to get back to the Marine Corps, but having him home is so wonderful, and my heart is full. I sleep better at night. So you keep him as busy as you can. Maybe he'll remember why he loves it here and stay."

"There's nothing here for me, Ma. Dad is running the ranch, and I'm in the way. Cricket's running the paper and I have no interest in that. My time with the Marines isn't done. That's where I'm supposed to be."

Mrs. Hannigan rolled her eyes.

Ellie returned the squeeze to Shane's hand. "Well, Grams and I are happy we can fill your time while you're here." She twisted her hand to remove it from Shane's grasp.

There was very little she disliked more than being a charity case, but it would seem being a distraction to make the time go by faster was just as distasteful.

SHANE DROVE Ellie home in silence, her head against the cool window, feigning exhaustion. Truth was, she was very tired. Not only was she trying to figure out who was doing all these dreadful things to her and the farm, but now she had the complication of her attraction to Shane to deal with. Shane, who was leaving. Which fine, okay, go. But don't bat her around like a cat playing with a mouse just for fun.

Being a mouse sucked.

"You're awfully quiet, cute-face."

"I'm ready for some sleep." She let her face stretch into a wide yawn. "Your parents are very nice."

"They like you."

Not that it matters, she wanted to say. *Or who cares?* Once he left, she would have no connection to them. She'd only see them at town functions, and maybe not even then.

He brushed his hand down her arm, then caressed her cheek. She turned her face more toward the glass.

"Ellie." He sighed. "Wanna tell me what's bugging you?"

"Nothing is bugging me." What a relief when they'd turned onto the drive leading to the farm.

"Seriously?" He sounded like he was going to laugh. "Your body language says otherwise."

Ellie mumbled, "My *body language* says I'm tired."

"Too tired to make out?"

Incredulous, she sat straight up and faced him. "Are you kidding?"

"Now I have your attention," he said. "Tell me what's bothering you."

The farm was in sight, everything looked to be okay, and she nearly sighed with relief. She needed to get away from Shane because part of her really did want to make out. Once he'd mentioned it, she'd started coming up with fantasies. Darn him.

She undid her seat belt and picked up her purse. "There is nothing to talk about." She put her hand on the latch to open the door. When he was close enough to the front porch, she was going to get out, even if she had to tuck and roll her way out of the SUV.

"Ellie, something has upset you and I want to know what." He slowed the SUV in front of the house, preparing to come to a stop.

Ellie pulled the latch then jumped from the SUV.

"Ellie," he called out.

She walked to the front door as fast as she could without running and didn't turn around.

"Why you running away if nothing's wrong?" was the last thing she heard before slamming the house door behind her.

12

SUNDAY

The next morning Shane waited for Ellie outside the farmhouse. He sat on her tailgate and considered the plugs in his hands.

She came out, stumbled when she saw him, then sighed. She looked like he felt, that a quality night of sleep had escaped her. Sleep had escaped him. He'd spent most of the night considering his options. Which weren't many. Staying here in Wolf Creek meant no job at the ranch, and going back to the Marines likely meant a lifetime job as an instructor.

He showed her the plugs in his hands.

"What are those?"

"They are the little devices that have been letting the air out of your tires. I found two of them in. One inserted in the front driver's tire and the other the back passenger tire."

"Again?" She slapped her hands against her legs in frustration. "I wish we knew who was doing this. I'd go directly to them right now and punch them in the face. Twice."

"That would be fun to see." He gestured to her truck. "They

weren't there when I dropped you off. I checked. But they've been in there long enough that you lost too much air to drive. So they must have put them in after I left."

Ellie pressed her palms to her eyes, likely pushing back tears, and said in a watery voice, "I can't do this much longer."

Shane stood and went to her. He wrapped her in a hug. "We'll figure this out. We just need to look outside the box. But for now, I'll take you to work."

She leaned against him, her hands to her sides, her forehead against his shoulder. "If they put them in after you dropped me off, does that mean they were here watching? Or could it be a coincidence?"

"I'm not a believer in coincidences." He rubbed her back.

"Me either, and thinking they were watching the house gives me the creeps." She shuddered and stepped closer to him. Maybe she wasn't mad at him anymore. He considered asking again if she wanted to make out, but thought he'd better not. He'd save the idea for later when she wasn't scared.

"The others are meeting us at the diner after your shift. We need to rally the troops. We need some more eyes on the situation." He kissed her temple. "Come on, buck up. If they're watching you right now, then they know they've rattled your cage."

Ellie stiffened and stepped out of his arms. She whispered, "Do you think they might be?"

Shane shrugged. "Possible. Nearly ninety percent of my job is to wait and watch. I can't image whoever is doing this could get lucky all the time. They have to know your routine. They have to know lots about you and Grams."

Ellie paled and bit her lip.

Okay, now she looked terrified, and Shane couldn't have that. He closed the small space between them and put his hands on her upper arms. "Don't let them see you scared, cute-face."

"But I *am* scared. It's all I can think about." Her bottom lip quivered.

"Think about this instead." He jerked her toward him and delivered a deep, searing kiss. Ellie moaned and melted into him. Her tongue met his without hesitation. Their kiss was energized, fueled by their deep desire for one another and a little from her fear. When they broke apart, both were breathing heavily.

"You taste yummy. A little like coffee and a whole lot like cream," he murmured against her temple.

"I drink my coffee black," she said.

"I wasn't talking about that cream. I bet if I took you to bed, you would rock my world. And man, I really want to find out if that's true."

"Shut up," she said and wrapped her arms around his neck. "You're ruining the moment, and I *so* need this moment."

The message was clear. He kissed her again, harder, skimming his hands over her ribs, then moving up to cover her breast. She pressed into him.

"If we keep this up, you won't make it to the diner," he promised, then bent his knees so he could kiss under her chin.

She sighed woefully then stepped away. "I should really go to work. All those hungry people. Especially after the early morning church service."

"Maybe we should do this a few minutes more in case your creeper is watching,"

Ellie narrowed her eyes. "Did you kiss me because you thought we might be watched?"

"No, I kissed you because I couldn't help myself. Having your creeper watch is a bonus."

Ellie grimaced. "I'm not sure which is creepier. You faking attraction to me or getting off on being watched."

Shane snatched her hand and pressed it to his groin. "Does that feel like I'm faking attraction?" He was hard as a ginormous redwood.

Ellie snatched back her hand and slapped him on the shoulder again, but laughed. Her cheeks tinted pink. "You say the crudest things."

He leaned toward her. "And you like it."

She gasped, her eyes widening. "I think I kinda do," she said with a groan.

Shane threw back his head and barked out a laugh. He tossed an arm around her shoulder and guided her to his truck.

"For the record, I don't get off on being watched. You do this to me. But it's a double bonus if whoever is targeting you sees us and maybe reconsiders their position with me around. Know what I'm saying?"

"I suppose."

He opened the door for her and waited for her to climb in the truck. "Whoever is doing this is working around me. I take heart in knowing there haven't been any more fences down, baited trails, or snakes. They've gone back to inconveniencing you."

"No snakes or fence troubles that we have *yet*, but give it another few days. This hasn't played out."

After climbing in the driver's side, Shane gave her knee an encouraging squeeze. "We'll get it fixed."

"I know. Only my gut says it's going to get worse before it gets better."

Funny thing. His did, too.

AFTER HER SHIFT, Ellie took a bowl of oatmeal to the corner round table where Cricket, Sabrina, Bryce, Hannah, and Cori sat waiting. Shane led Grams into the diner and to the group. He'd gone to the farm to put air in her tires and collect Grams.

Hannah had her computer and was typing madly.

"How you doing?" Ellie asked Cori, pointing to her large baby bump. She made a mental note to finish the baby blanket and carrier set before Cori popped. Which looked to be coming up soon.

"No complaints. Best part is eating whatever I want, whenever I want." Cori smiled and stabbed a fork-load of chocolate chip pancakes.

"You ate whatever you wanted *before* you were pregnant," Sabrina said. She and Cori had known each other since they were young adults, both having grown up in Texas.

"Yeah, but now, everyone overlooks it because of the baby. Before people must have thought I had an out of control tapeworm." Cori ate another bite.

Sabrina nodded in agreement. "True."

Cori pointed her fork at Ellie. "Fort wanted me to tell you he has no leads on anything, that his role in this case is useless."

Ellie laughed then returned to eating her breakfast.

Bryce scoffed. "I bet he didn't say that, Cori." He was a loyal friend.

"No, that was me paraphrasing." She looked to Shane. "Oh, and there have been other coyote issues. He wants you to come talk to him about possibly hunting them. Still a concern that one might have rabies."

"Bryce and I went out one night and I went out a second but no trail of any coyotes. I did see mountain lion tracks." Shane raised his brows. "That might be our predator."

Bryce leaned over the table and said in a lowered voice, "But let's keep that to ourselves rights now. If word gets out, it'll cause some chaos. We want to make sure first before we sound the alarms."

Shane nodded. "Will do."

Ellie ran a finger over her lips, indicating they were sealed.

"How are things going with you two?" Sabrina asked.

"What do you mean?" Shane and Ellie asked in unison. Ellie was staring at her oatmeal.

"I mean with figuring out what's behind all this? And working together. Have you been able to make it look like there might be something between you two?" Sabrina asked.

Hm, let's see. They'd made out on the ground next to a dead rattlesnake, they'd kissed and groped each other this morning in front of the house. To Ellie, that was a yes.

She glanced at Shane who winked at her. She purposefully did not look at Grams. "Eh, we're doing what we can." She thought of the conversation this morning. "We don't know if anyone is around to see it."

"Have the incidents decreased?" Bryce asked.

Shane answered, "Hard to say." He told them about the tire plugs and rattlesnakes, leaving interpretation to whether the incidents had slowed up to the individual.

"You both need to step up the game," Sabrina said.

"Yeah, totally. You need to go out and be seen." This from Cricket.

"I agree," Grams added.

"We went to Mom and Dad's last night," Shane told her.

"Oh, well that's good enough," Cricket said and rolled her eyes. "No, you need to be seen here, canoodling."

Everyone looked at Cricket.

"Canoodling?" Cori asked. "How old *are* you?"

Cricket tossed her hand in the air in frustration then pointed at Shane. "Well, he's my brother. I don't want to tell him he needs to be getting it on with my friend. And with her grandmother here who, by the way, was my Sunday school teacher. It's weird. Especially if they don't really like each other and they're just pretending."

"I don't dislike him," Ellie said.

"I'm not pretending," Shane said at the same time.

Silence filled the air. Everyone was looking at her and Shane, and she desperately wanted to run from the diner. Lord, it was embarrassing. Shane put a hand on her knee and squeezed. He was a steady calm in her chaotic world.

Sabrina broke the silence. "I think Cricket is right. Go on some dates." She put "dates" in air quotes. "Be seen in town. Make people think there's something there."

"I don't think that's going to stop this person. If we can figure out their motivation, we might be able to get ahead of them." Shane shook his head in frustration. "But we know nothing. I'm just the guy who comes and goes, and they're working around that."

"Then stay," Cori said.

"Get married," Sabrina said.

"What?" Ellie and Shane said together in surprise.

Cori waved away their shock. "That's her default. She tries to get everyone married."

Sabrina smiled and said, "Sometimes when people are meant to be"––she shrugged—"getting married is the next step. It doesn't matter where it comes in the sequence because they'll have the same obstacles married or not. Married, they're a united front."

Grams wagged at finger at Ellie. "She has a point. Your granddad and I met and married within two months. I wouldn't change a thing. I knew he was for me the moment I saw him."

"But that's not us, Grams. We aren't meant to be," Ellie said. She pointed to Shane. "He's meant to be shooting guns somewhere—"

"With the Marines. And she's meant to be coddling goats," Shane finished.

Ellie narrowed her eyes and glared at him. "I do more than coddle goats."

"I only meant you are supposed to be here. I'm supposed to be somewhere else," Shane said.

Cricket shook her head. "That's not true. You're supposed to be here. You've always planned on coming back. Only now its happened earlier than you scheduled. You have to adjust."

Grams thumped the table. "This is all very interesting, but my hearing aid has a limited window of working ability. I'm about to reach it, and soon it'll start screeching obnoxiously. So, back to the point. We don't know who is doing this. We can't even come up with a list of suspects that's not our friends and neighbors. Not much has changed, so my solution is that we should change."

Everyone's gaze darted from one person to the other, as each person was waiting for the other to speak next. Shane and Bryce were nodding.

"What's your solution, Mrs. Greene?" Shane asked.

"I think you should stay over. You seeing how we live might trigger something we don't realize." Grams crossed her arms over her chest. "But you'll have to tell me if that's a good idea soon." She tapped her hearing aid. "Tick, tick."

"Its a great idea," Cricket, Cori, and Sabrina said.

Everyone looked at Hannah.

"Why are you so quiet?" her husband, Bryce asked.

"Because I've built a spreadsheet that will help us look at probability." She spun her computer around. "We need to add some names to it and some data in other fields, like frequency of interactions, and see what the spreadsheet tells us. If that means Shane has to have a sleepover to get the info, fine."

Ellie lifted her hand slightly. "Technically, I'm the one having the sleepover. Me and Grams."

Grams laughed right as her hearing aid began to screech. She took it out with a mumble of unintelligible words. "Stupid things." Grams looked around the diner. "Look, there's Lester Phillips. Man only gets a decent meal when he eats out. I'm gonna invite him over." Grams pushed from the table and approached Phillips.

"Lester," she fairly yelled, "when's the last time you had dinner at our house?"

"Too long, Minnie. Far too long." Mr. Phillips jumped from his seat and moved at lightning speed to pull out a chair for Grams.

Cricket leaned toward Shane and Ellie, bringing Ellie's attention back to the topic at hand. Shane staying the night.

Cricket said, "Grams may be there, but it'll be Ellie who has to entertain on her first co-ed sleepover. Whatever will you do?" She wagged her brows.

Ellie nearly upchucked her breakfast.

13

SUNDAY

Shane showed up that evening with a duffle bag slung over his right shoulder and a cocky grin on his face. Dressed like always, dark jeans, boots, hat, and a flannel shirt, Ellie wondered if he slept in dark pajamas too. Or maybe he slept in nothing.

Today she would know.

Maybe.

Ugh.

She needed to stop thinking about Shane in less clothing. And Shane in no clothing. Or simply stop thinking about Shane at all and keep her head in the game. She was trying to grow her business, not get laid.

Ellie squelched a giggle. Getting laid wouldn't be awful. Her past was limited to one guy, Boring Brad. She'd heard talk of this myth known as great sex and wanted to know if good sex really existed.

She mentally slapped herself upside the head.

"Come in, Shane," Grams said and waved him into the living room. "Dinner is almost ready."

Ellie took his duffle bag and put it on the stairs. "I'll show you your room later."

"Is it your room?" he whispered.

Ellie chose to ignore him. She knew he was teasing her.

"Grams and I were talking about her going to visit her sister, my Aunt Hattie. She lives in Florida." Ellie sat on the couch and tucked her legs under her. Benny, without his jet, was sleeping on the cushion next to her.

"Are you going?" Shane asked and sat on the other side of Benny.

"Bah," Grams said and fiddled with her ear. "Do I strike you as a woman who likes to be hot all the time?" She was dressed in a T-shirt even though the weather outside was brisk enough for a jacket. "And Hattie talks about the lizards and roaches that fly. No thanks. I like it here. Everyone keeps trying to get me to Florida. Ellie's dad Paul, Hattie, even Landry has suggested it. You see anyone else packing up and going to Florida?"

Ellie shook her head. "Don't get all worked up, Grams. You know they're only saying it because they worry about you being lonely or working too hard."

Minnie plopped in her Lazy-boy, then kicked the recliner back while reaching for her knitting. "They can all go to hell. I don't tell them what to do, but I sure could with Paul."

Shane laughed. "Do they all know about what's going on?"

"Not my dad. I haven't been specific. I might have mentioned the tires and irrigation." Ellie looked at Grams. "Have you said anything?"

"Your dad doesn't talk to me. He knows he can't boss me around like he tries with you so he doesn't even bother."

"Your dad is bossy?" Shane asked.

"Isn't everyone's dad? He just wants me to be happy." Ellie stroked Benny's head.

Minnie's hand moved deftly, the needles clicking loudly, punctuating her irritation. "Trouble is, Paul thinks others' happiness has to look identical to his definition of it. Never met such a shortsighted man in my life. How he came from and Earl, I'll never know."

Ellie gave a shrug and whispered to Shane, "My dad *really* irritates her."

"Where's your mom in all this?" Shane started petting Benny, too.

Ellie snorted. "She does whatever my dad wants. She used to be a nurse, wanted to specialize in head injuries, but then she met my dad, had me, and now she lives in the jungle or desert or wherever my dad wants to be."

"Which is why my Ellie is paving her own path. Ain't no man gonna dictate where she goes and what she does with her dreams," Grams said and winked at Ellie.

Ellie faced Shane. "I need this farm to work, Shane. I failed out of college, twice. This is what I want to do. This is home and how I want to live. Someone is trying to take that away from us."

Shane cocked his head. "Mrs. Greene—"

"Call me Grams, honey."

"Has anyone done anything to you?" Shane sat forward, resting his elbows on his knees and working out a thought that he'd been bothering over the past few days. "You run the farm stand in the mornings, right? Anything gone wrong there?"

Grams's needles paused as she thought. "Well, let me see." She shook her head. "I can't think of anything. Nothing that doesn't sit right. Nothing broken or weird. Sometimes a bit of produce will go missing, but I figured it was someone hungry."

Shane asked, "Explain to me what each of you do on the farm. I think I have an idea about what Ellie does, but I might be missing something."

"Grams does the mornings at the farm stand, and she waters the crops. Since our pivot irrigation is broken and we've run hose sprinklers down the rows, Grams has to manually hook them up one at a time."

"It's a pain in the ass is what it is," Grams said, her needles clacking again. "If I start earlier, I can get most of the watering done by two. Ellie's to figure out something with timers."

"I'd like to get the irrigation working again," Ellie mumbled.

"I'll look at it tomorrow," Shane said. "What I'm hearing is the trouble is isolated to what Ellie takes care of? Right?"

Grams's needles stopped moving. "I hadn't thought of that."

The dinging of a timer came from the kitchen.

Ellie stood up, arms wrapped around her body. "Lasagna's done. Not that I'm hungry anymore."

The dinner conversation was about everything but the farm's troubles and Ellie being the target. Until Grams excused herself and went off to bed. Shane and Ellie were sitting at the kitchen table, coffee and the remains of a banana cream pie between them.

He grabbed the seat of her chair and pulled it closer to his. He then dropped his arm across the back of her chair and leaned closer to her. "I can tell this isn't sitting right with you. Thinking you're the target, but its giving us a direction to go in. We could be wrong, and that would be great, but it eliminates people and narrows the field." He looked pointedly at her, asking if she understood what he was saying. He didn't want her to panic yet.

"What if it is me, and I'm making Grams life worse? That will destroy me. She's taken me in, this is my home, and I might be why the farm she's spent her life to create is being destroyed." Ellie buried her head in Shane's shoulder.

"Part of what makes this so hard is the feeling you have no control." He rubbed her back. "I know making a list of suspects has been hard. Let's start with making a list of everyone you come into contact with. Tomorrow I have more scouting to do for Fort. I can stop by some of the ranches and feel out some of the people on the list."

Ellie straightened. "Won't that be dangerous?"

"Cute-face, I'm a sniper for the Marine Corps. I think that tops this." He kissed her temple.

"Too right." Ellie yawned. "I'll make a list tonight and give it to you. Do you mind if we call it a night? I'm beat."

"Point me in the direction of your room." Shane pushed from the table and pulled out her chair as well.

"I know you say that like you mean it, but I think its bluster. I can't see you taking advantage of me with Grams in the house." She looked up into his face and smiled while she let her ponytail out, then rubbed her fingers over her scalp. Maybe she wanted to test him. Push him into taking the first step, the one she was too chicken to take.

He stepped closer until their bodies were a hairsbreadth away. "Wanna try me?"

Ellie moaned. Her fingers stilled.

"Is that moan for me or the massage you're giving yourself." He looked too pleased with himself.

"The massage, definitely that," she baited.

He pulled gently at her forearms, bringing her hands out of her hair and to her sides. Then he backed her two steps until she bumped into the wall. He pressed the length of himself to her. "Are you sure?"

Ellie squeaked.

Shane let go of her arms and stepped away with a chuckle. "I can live with that." He held out his hand. "Come on, you have bags under your eyes, and tomorrow is another long day. Show me to my room."

When she took his hand, he pulled her forward and then past him until she was in the lead. Then he gave her a friendly shove toward the stairs. Ellie laughed. On the way up, he grabbed his duffle bag. She assumed the bag was heavy because his step was heavier on one side. The stairs opened up at the center of the second floor. The main bathroom was straight ahead. Two doors sat to the right and left of the bathroom.

"Obviously, that's the bathroom," she told him. "There are towels on your bed."

Ellie pointed to the left and the farthest door at the end of the hallway. "That's Grams's room." She then pointed to the door between Grams's room and the bathroom. "That's me, if you need anything." She turned right and led him down the hall to the last door.

She showed him the guest room, which used to be her father's. The room was large with a window-seat bench. It faced east and captured the morning sun. It was the room farthest from Grams.

"Roger." He stood in the doorway of his room.

Ellie backed down the hallway. "I'll be in here if you need anything." She almost tripped over her own feet, but caught herself by pressing a hand to the wall. "Good night." She turned and fled. She heard Shane chuckle as she closed the door and then leaned against it.

Cripes, he made her so nervous. And excited. And hot and sweaty. Ellie fanned herself while she kicked off her shoes. Her focus fell on the desk in the corner of the room, a stack of bills piled in the center.

She needed to think of something other than Shane Hannigan, and making a list would be the perfect distraction. She couldn't very well go to sleep with Shane on her mind. It would be one restless night. Of course, going to sleep with her last thought about who might be out to get her wouldn't guarantee a good night sleep either. But of the two, bad dreams were easier to get over than sexual ones. Those type of dreams liked to revisit and always left her hot and bothered for hours after.

Ellie moved to her desk and found a scrap piece of paper and a pen buried under the bills. She wrote the number one and then was at a loss. Who should she put on the list? Shane had said to put people she came in contact with, but she knew it was a suspect list.

She heard Shane in the bathroom and lost her train of thought. Her mind filled with images of his broad chest and bulky arms. Jeez, she was such a sucker for a good body. Or maybe it was just *his* good body. The press of his hard chest against hers had filled her mind with a montage of images of what his body might look like. He was, after all, a fit Marine, and she'd once seen a calendar of hot Marines. Was Shane buff like them?

He shuffled back to his room, and then his door squeaked closed.

Ellie pursed her lips, a thought percolating. If she timed her next move *just right,* she might catch him with his shirt off but pants still on. *So* not inappropriate at all. She looked at the paper in her hand. Well, she did need help figuring out this list, after all.

Before she could talk herself out of getting her cheap thrill, Ellie dashed out of her room and down the hall, her stocking feet quiet on the wood floors. She knocked once, and then while turning the doorknob, she pushed against the door. "Shane, do you have a second? Are you decent?"

"Don't come in," Shane shouted.

But Ellie was already in motion. The door swung open and, sure as goat shit, Shane was sitting on the edge of the bed with nothing on but running shorts. Also, his lower leg was standing next to him, boot still on. The bedside lamp was the only light illuminating the room so half his face was cast in shadows.

Ellie stared at his pecs and licked her lips. He was better than a hot Marine calendar picture. He was the real deal. Those guys in the calendar were oiled up. Shane was rugged, yet smooth, with a smattering of dark hair across his chest that faded into his nether region.

Ellie was a dumbass. Her sneak peek left her wanting to see more. She wanted to follow that fading hair trail to what lay beyond. Like a mystery begging to be solved.

"Ellie. I...ah...." He shook his head. "You need to get out." His voice was low and steely.

Something was off. She knew she'd overlooked something key. Besides, she never figured Shane for being a prude, and he seemed angry, caught off guard at her interruption. Not at all how she expected. She thought he'd jump at the opportunity to have her in his room. Her gaze swept down his body to the missing portion below the knee. Then swung to the prosthetic next to him. Bam! She saw it now. His leg came in two parts.

Her mouth fell open, and she slapped herself on the forehead, the paper in her hand briefly covering her face. "That totally makes sense. Why didn't I realize it? I mean, with the goats—"

"I am not one of your damn goats to be coddled." His voice was cold and hard. "Now kindly get out." He pointed one finger at her and then to the space behind her.

"I didn't say anything about you being one of my goats. And if I coddle its because its in my nature. So don't yell at me. I don't see why you're being such as ass." She put her hands on her hips.

"I don't need you or anyone feeling sorry for me. Or thinking I can't do something." Shane pointed again to the space behind her.

"Wow," Ellie said incredulously. "Why would I think that?" She pointed to herself. "Look at me. Do I look like I feel sorry for you? We live in a time where technology is amazing. Even my goats have prosthesis. Goats! If you're seeing pity from me, it's because you're an idiot and I'm sad to realize that's the case." She didn't care if he had a prosthetic leg. Why would or should she? She barely noticed to be honest. What she did notice, however, was the way his arms bulked and flexed as he moved them. She'd caught glimpses when he was working outside, but shirtless... She bit her lip.

Shane's eyes narrowed. "What did you want, Ellie. What made you burst in here so rudely?" When he crossed his arms over her chest, his pec muscles jumped. Ellie's knees wobbled, and heat rushed through her body.

"I wanted to know..." She let the paper flutter to the floor as she walked toward him. "I wanted to see your chest." She stopped directly in front of him.

He dropped his arms, resting his hands on either side of him. "Well, you're seeing it. What are you going to do about it?" She knew it was a challenge. She also knew he was expecting her to run. She figured if she did, he would attribute it to his prosthetic leg. As if injuries like that would put her off? He really did underestimate her.

She swept her gaze over him, desperate to touch everything she saw. "I'm going to show you mine." She whipped of her T-shirt.

He sucked in a deep breath, and she reveled in the pleasure that she caught him off guard.

"Ellie, what are you doing?" he whispered.

She stepped between his knees. "I don't know."

"Are you going to run away if I touch you?" He met her gaze and stared hard, daring her to have courage, to stick it out.

She shook her head. "No, but its taking so long for you to touch me, and now you've planted *that* seed to run in my head—"

He reached out and grabbed at her waist, tugging her closer. "I don't know if I'll be able to stop."

"I don't know if I'll want you to." She released her worries, her fears, and her tendency to overthink everything and grasped the moment, clutched it greedily in her cupped palms. She put her hands on his shoulders and caressed down his chest. Then ran them up again.

"You've got to give me something here, cute-face, something that tells me you're not going to leave me high and dry." His hands, still on her waist allowed him to caress her stomach, his thumbs making gentle strokes.

"How about this?" she said and pushed him down onto the bed. She climbed up and straddled him. His hand came around to her ass, cupping it, pulling her up on him. She unclasped her bra and let it fall to the side.

"This is going to be fun," he said before leaning forward and taking one breast in his mouth.

"It's been a long time since I had any fun," she said and gave herself over to him.

Sex with Shane was not "fit item A into slot B." That's what she'd been expecting. Instead, he touched her with gentle hands, kissed her with soft lips, held her in an embrace that felt like he never wanted to let go. He made it easy for her to get lost in him and let her troubles slip away.

When Shane put his mouth anywhere on her, Ellie came alive. She felt everything right down to the last nerve ending. She sizzled from the kinetic energy of their bodies brushing against each other, their hands gripping and caressing. He touched her like a starving man might, seeking to quench a hunger she felt, too. Both loved the night away as if this might be the only chance they'd get. They fit together. Not just physically, but emotionally, too. She didn't have to hold back her need for him. Her energy for more, her demands, verbal and not, didn't give him pause. With Shane, she was who she always wanted to be—the farm girl making her life happen one day at time, and she'd made this moment happen, too. And then she'd made it happen twice more.

MONDAY

S hane was both exhausted and rejuvenated. Ellie had worked him hard the night before. The aftermath had left him infused with something he hadn't known was missing. Touch, companionship, and a deeper connection to another person. He'd lived his life by keeping his distance, watching the days go by through a riflescope. The adrenaline rush he got from his job was unlike any other, until now.

Sex with Ellie was heady business, a different type of high. He hadn't expected it. When she'd climbed on top and rode him hard and fast, the euphoria nearly broke him. He'd had casual sex before, and this wasn't it. Shane couldn't identify why, just yet. He figured the familiarity of their sex had more to do with him being home, surrounded by friends, and in his comfort zone.

At first, he'd thought when she'd come on to him it was because she saw his missing limb. He assumed she would stroke his head and rub under his chin like she did her little special needs goats. But she'd done the opposite. She didn't touch him because she thought he needed it; she'd touched him because she needed it. She'd made that clear in her actions and words, with her greedy hands and mouth. She'd given and taken in equal measures. Without a second glance at his missing limb.

Shane smiled from his good fortune. Here he'd been, all broody about waiting out his med board. Ellie definitely had made the days easier to get through. Shane arched on his mount, a Rocky Mountain Horse named Joe, and let out a yawn while he stretched. When he'd gotten up before dawn and with Ellie, he'd checked her truck for tampering, then followed her to the diner. After which he'd driven home, hooked up the horse trailer, retrieved Joe, and took an old but well-traveled hunting road that led deep led into the forest toward the foothills of the Bighorn's. Here he would begin scouting for signs of a rabid coyote, or whatever, and work his way down toward the ranches.

The first name on Ellie's suspect list was Mr. Phillips. Phillips owned the ranch to the south of the Greenes' farm. He was a Vietnam veteran and a conspiracy theorist of the highest form. Phillips, like many in Wolf Creek, had suffered losses with the wildfires last spring. Shane figured Phillips was a good place to start. Maybe a motive would be found. Especially if it was true he'd been uninsured at the time of the fires

The Tetons lay to the west of Wolf Creek, Bighorn National Forest to the east. Shane was riding south, the majestic landscapes to each side. The trapped feeling that typically engulfed him when surrounded by the mountains was nowhere to be found. Shane sat back in the saddle and let all the tension and worries ease from him. Since the explosion that threw him from the Humvee transporting him back to base and the second that took away his leg, Shane had been holding on to what would become of him. Who was he without the Marines? Everyday not knowing was killing him. Except...the past few days he hadn't checked his phone obsessively, looking for a missed call or an email. These past few days he'd been living in the present, not worrying about the future.

The terrain gradually turned dry. Joe's steps kicked up more dust the farther south Shane rode. Where once green pastures covered the land, a fire had swiped clean, replaced with red dirt.

New growth and sagebrush were popping up everywhere, but patches of the land looked barren and harsh. Small rocks jutted from the soil ready to poke and bruise. Shane wiped his brow and glanced up at the sun, bright and warm. Not a cloud in the sky. He rolled his shoulders back and took in a restorative breath. Like him, the earth was scarred. And also like him, it was healing, and the rebirth looked to be just as promising.

This of course meant many of the landmarks he'd used in the past to find his way were gone. Shane had to rely on instinct and his internal sense of distance to know when to fork off toward Phillips's small shotgun-style ranch. He'd brought a GPS just in case but was game to see if his muscle memory was still good or if the concussion he suffered in the bombing had knocked it out of whack.

A few miles farther, and he veered off in the direction of Phillips house. No signs of any coyote scat. Or mountain lion, for that matter. Shane figured if the wild animal in question was real, there was no telling which direction it might come from. Both the Tetons and Bighorn forest were alive and strong. Looked like he was hard-up for clues on two fronts; the rogue animal and what was happening to Ellie.

He rode through a small herd of Angus where no more than twenty were grazing. The brand on the flank told Shane these were Phillips's cattle. Shane rode into the yard of the house, but Phillips was nowhere to be found.

Outside Phillips's house sat a water trough, and attached to the top was a bell. He left Joe to drink from the trough and gave the bell a ring. Shane had to hand it to Phillips. His old-school way of thinking, like using the trough, was clever. Shane bet lots of cowboys, ranch hands, and ranchers knew the trough was there. Stopping to let their horses drink opened up the opportunity to chat. Chatting lead to information, all garnered while Phillips sat on his front porch.

A shrill whistle came from Shane's left, and he turned and saw Phillips coming from the barn fifty feet away. Behind the barn, twelve wood stakes with waving orange flags marked out a small square plot of land where the earth had been turned.

Phillips raised a hand in greeting. "What brings you out this way?" he shouted.

Shane shifted his weight off his prosthetic and waited for Phillips to get closer. The older man was wearing coveralls, was covered in sawdust, and a hammer hung from the loop on the side of his pants. A cigarillo in the corner of his mouth.

"I was asked by Sheriff Besingame and Game and Fish to help out with a wildlife issue. Stopped by to see if you might be having any problems." Damn if Shane wasn't finding pleasure in the day. He was enjoying the ride, chatting with the ranchers, and being a part of his community. He enjoyed being useful.

"Come on up to the porch. I got cold stuff in a cooler up there." Phillips waved him toward the house and headed that way himself.

Phillips's house faced east and still bore signs from the fire. Large dark streaks of soot stained one side, showing how close the fire had come. Two old wicker chairs sat on a porch that ran the length of half the house, small portions of their seats missing as the wicker had given way to overuse.

Shane followed and stretched out in the nearest chair. He took off his Stetson, and after pulling a bandana from his pocket, wiped his head. He plopped the hat back on.

Phillips opened an old weather-beaten, faded-red Coleman cooler and offered Shane a soda.

Taking the soda, Shane said, "This is quite the setup. I might make it a point to come by more often."

Phillips chuckled, causing his unlit cigarillo that clung to his dry bottom lip to bounce. He sat in the chair beside him. "That's not something I hear every day. So I'm guessing you're looking for a coyote. Must be a bad one. What's he got or what's he done?"

Shane shook his head. He wasn't about to share anything more than he had to with Phillips. The man was a known gossip. "Don't know for sure. Just rumors and speculation. Coyote might not even exist."

"But there's been some trouble. Is it the same coyote that went after Ellie's little Benny?"

Shane surveyed Phillips. "How'd you hear about that?"

"Same way I reckon everyone did. Minnie. I stopped by the farm stand for some beets. I like them pickled, eat them right out of the jar. Trouble is, the pickling process is a pain in my bum leg. Reckon you know what I mean about that." Phillips bent forward and pulled up the pant on his right leg. Half the calf muscle was gone. "Shrapnel. Burns like a bitch sometimes to this day. Doc says its all in my mind, but why would anyone want to re-experience feeling pain like that?"

Shane gave a wry smile. He could commiserate. He pulled up the jeans of his left leg and showed Phillips his prosthesis. One combat vet to the other.

Phillips whistled. "That's a beaut. Can't tell with the jeans down that its not real."

"It comes with other attachments. One for running, one for swimming."

"I'll be damned. We've come a long way from wooden peg legs." Phillips winked.

Shane laughed. "Thankfully. I'm surprised you don't think this is alien technology." He nettled the man just a little. Was Phillips quick to anger?

Phillips slapped his hand on his knee and laughed. He then said, "What makes you think I don't think its alien technology? You've seen some of those doctors out there. They're too stupid to come up with something that creative."

It was Shane's turn to laugh. There were many days in the

hospital and rehab he'd have liked to put his fist in a doctor's face. What did the white coat know-it-all understand about pain sustained in combat when he'd been in a safe hospital the entire time, drinking his fancy coffees and watching endless channels on cable TV?

Shane leaned forward and pointed to the stub. "Sometimes, right here I get this searing pain that makes me see white lights. It used to be so intense it would make me almost vomit." He pulled his jeans down. "But it's getting better."

"Hate to tell you, it'll never go away." Phillips lifted the lid of the cooler and offered another drink. Shane shook his head.

"You were saying Mrs. Greene told you about Benny?" Not the subtlest of reentries back to the initial conversation, but hey, he didn't have all day.

"Yeah, she told me about the broken gate lock and the coyote getting in." Phillips crushed his can and tossed it in the cooler then selected another drink. "This was after she sold me the beets and came over to help me pickle them." Phillips flashed a happy smile.

"You wouldn't know anything about that, would you?"

Phillips looked at him, brow digging down slightly. "About the lock? Nope, I checked it after Ellie installed it, but that girl doesn't need anyone to go behind her, checking her work. She's got it covered."

"She is awfully handy," Shane agreed.

"I'm glad you're hanging out there, though. Must say, I do drive-bys just to make sure everything's okay. Did Ellie tell you their irrigation broke down?"

Shane nodded.

"Well, it broke down because someone took a hammer to it and broke it down."

Shane straightened. "You mean to say—"

"Yeah, on purpose. And that's not the only shit going wrong out there. I was out there for dinner a week or so ago, and when I left, I saw someone had stuck a pin in Ellie's front tire, letting all the air out." Phillips shook his head then spat on the ground. "Only way I found it was 'cause I heard the tire hissing."

Shane tried to keep a poker face. He had no way of knowing if Phillips was playing him or not. More importantly, he wanted to know why Ellie hadn't said anything about his. "What did Ellie say when she saw it?"

Phillips met his stare. "I didn't tell her. Not about either. She called me over and asked why the pivot irrigation wasn't working. That's when I saw someone had broken off the valves. As for her tire, well, I took out the pin and tossed it in the garbage. I went back into the house and told her about her tire being low and to get air in it first thing in the morning. I went to the diner that morning, and she'd taken care of it."

Shane asked the next obvious question. "Who do you think did it?"

Phillips rubbed his knees with his palms. "How would I know? Your generation takes dating as serious as a gnat. No such thing as a steady in you all's world. I figured she'd made some fella mad, and now that you're around, that should nip it in the butt."

"Bud," Shane muttered.

"Come again?" Phillips held a hand to his right ear.

"Nothing," Shane said. He didn't correct him about the butt nipping because nothing had been nipped in the bud or the butt.

"You take old-timers like Minnie and me. We dated with intention. We married for life. Well, Minnie did. I'm still looking for the right woman. Tell me who wouldn't want some of this?" Phillips spread his hands wide to indicate his ranch.

"I dunno, sir. It's a nice piece of land. How you fixed since the fire?" Shane recalled what Cricket said about Phillips not having insurance.

Phillips pointed to the cattle. "I got enough food to sell for some extra cash and to keep me in steaks until my ticker decides to give out on me. Its how my dad and grandpa went. I figure it's not a stretch to assume I'll go the same. But it's no secret that fire hurt a lot of us. Between it and the cattle rustlers, it was a tough year, no doubt about it. But I don't ranch because it's easy. I reckon your dad's the same way."

"Yes, sir. He is." Shane gave the conversation some thought. Other than point blank asking, there was no way to know if Phillips was involved in the Greenes' farm problems. Even if Shane did ask, Phillips could easily lie. He caught sight of the orange flags. Shane gestured with his chin. "What's that about? If you don't mind me asking. You building something?"

Phillips chuckled. "Get this," he said and swat Shane on the shoulder. "After the fire, the land was pretty scorched. Came close to the house." He pointed to a visible line on the ground. One side of the line was fresh new growth but spotty with barren pockets, the other side, green-ish grass looked to make up Phillips's side yard. Yes, indeed, the fire had come within twenty yards of the house and barn according to the line.

Phillips continued, "Afterward, I was kicking around some rocks, trying to figure out what the hell I's gonna do. Over behind the barn, I kicked over some stuff and saw a nice little twinkle. Sure enough, it was gold. Not enough to put me in the riches, but enough to take the hurt out of the fire's aftermath. Know what I mean?"

Shane nodded like he did, even though he'd never been in Phillips's situation before.

"Couple weeks ago, these college students show up and ask if they can take a parcel of land and do some digging to see if there might be more goods there. They're paying me a fee for all my trouble." Phillips shrugged. "I figured why the hell not? Dig away."

Shane stored the information for later. "They find anything?"

Phillips shook his head. "I don't expect they will." He leaned forward like he was sharing a secret. "Fools don't realize that the fire changed the landscape, as did the heavy rains the season before. That gold was found in a boulder that could have rolled down from there." Phillips pointed his middle finger north toward the Greenes' land. "I expect these geniuses are looking in the wrong area." He chuckled again and slapped his knee. "But if they want to keep paying me to look, then I say be my guest."

Shane smiled. Lester Phillips was no fool. Shane glanced at the sun and confirmed the time by checking his watch.

He had one last question. "Who else knew about the gold?"

Phillips paused to give it some thought. "Well, just about anyone who would listen at the diner. Norris Landry hooked me up with some gold broker guy friend of his in Cody. I think this guy in Cody is how the students found out. If memory serves, the broker had to report it or something."

Another long trail that would likely lead to nowhere. "Well, its getting on. I best get going. I'm tracking an animal that might not even exist."

"You see a bigfoot out there or a unicorn, you come by here first and let me know. I'll split the winnings with you." Phillips followed Shane down off the porch and back into the yard.

"Bigfoot? I thought he was out in the Pacific Northwest." Shane took Joe's lead and gave the horse a rub on the muzzle.

"Nah, too much rain out there. Makes his hair get all mottled. I bet he's out here. And he has the hot springs to bathe in." Phillips fiddled with his hammer.

Shane didn't point out there were hot springs in the Pacific Northwest. "What are you making out there in the barn?" He nodded to the hammer. "Or are you fixing something? Need help?"

"Rat traps. Got me some big ones coming around and making a mess of things. Gonna trap 'em and take care of it myself." Phillips held out his hands approximately two feet apart. "Real big ones." He then gave a mock shiver. "Just showed up. People got a coyote problem and I got geology students and rodents. I'm not sure which of the two is better."

"Why don't you shoot them?" Shane mounted Joe. "The rats, not the students."

"Tried that. These mutant buggers seem to multiply every time you take one out. Now, I just want them off my property. See ya around, Shane." Phillips gave a wave.

"Thanks for the drink," Shane said. "If I see anything out there worth a call to Guinness book, I'll let you know." He smiled at the older man. It was going to be a damn shame if this old man was the one terrorizing Ellie. Shane liked Mr. Phillips.

Phillips touched a finger to his nose. "Between you and me."

With a wave, Shane road off to the northwest. Tomorrow he'd chat up someone else on Ellie's list. But first she'd have to add another name. Then after that, maybe he could get her to call out *his name* in pleasure.

MONDAY

Following his visit with Mr. Phillips, Shane rode back to his truck and horse trailer and drove Joe back to his family's ranch.

He texted Ellie and asked her to meet him in town at eight. Through the course of the day, he'd had an idea he couldn't get out of his head. So he was going to put it into action. All he needed was her to be willing.

She texted back: *Why eight? That's getting late.*

Who was she kidding about late? The sun wouldn't even be setting by then. He figured she'd be standoffish after the night they'd spent together. Shane wanted her to get beyond that. And he wanted another night. Oh so badly.

Please, he texted. *Come on, I promise you'll have a good time.*

He could almost hear her internal struggle as her response time grew longer. She was overthinking his choice of words "good time." He texted a little more for her to think about.

I have lots to tell you. Something to show you. And I want to see you outside of the farm. Sabrina said we should date and be seen.

Who will be in town at 8 for them to see us?

People at the bar. People in the diner. People who might have been hired to be a thorn in your side.

He waited. Then, impatient, typed, *We'll have a drink at the bar. When's the last time you did something to relax?*

Okay, she texted.

He let out the breath he'd been holding. He liked how determined she was. She didn't want to come out tonight, but she would. He also liked how dedicated she was, hardworking, sexy, loyal...and did he say sexy? Thinking about her all day had given him a woody.

Wear a skirt, please, he texted.

You wear a skirt!

I would, but then no one would notice you. And I want to see who pays you extra attention.

She sent an emoji that was rolling its eyes. Shane chuckled.

He showered, shaved his five o'clock shadow, checked his email, and then finally left for town.

Shane stopped by the sheriff's office before hitting up the diner for some dessert. He told Fort about what he saw, nothing, and they drafted a plan for the next day. Fort showed him a letter from the mayor and district head of Game and Fish. It was addressed to Shane and was formally offering him the job of Game and Fish Warden. With his degree in criminal science and a minor in environmental science, Shane was more than qualified for the job.

"There's been some attacks at the town east of ours. Tracks point toward Wolf Creek. Not that that means anything, but if it makes you compelled to take the job, then all the better."

Shane looked at the paper. "I don't know what to say. Officially, I'm still active duty."

"I know. I also know you're waiting on the med board. I wanted you to know this was an option. I figure the chance of getting you to stay here is slim, but options are a good thing to have, and I wanted you to have some." Fort tapped the paper.

"You'd be great at this. You have time to decide. Let us know what the board decides and what your plans are."

Shane nodded. "Will do."

"Until then, help me figure out what's going on with the wildlife. If I've got a coyote or a mountain lion out there or not."

The two men shook hands, and Shane left the office and headed to the diner, the offer folded in his breast pocket. When Ellie drove up, he was sitting on his tailgate waiting. In the truck's cab were some to-go sandwiches and chocolate cake. He was hoping they were going to work up an appetite later.

When she stepped out of her truck, Shane gave a whistle. She was a knockout. She wore a flowy black skirt with black cowboy boots, a white tank, and a hot pink gauzy shirt with the tails tied in a knot at her waist. The skirt showed off her legs that stretched for miles. He wanted to skip the bar and go straight to the following event. The one where he could get body-pressed-to-body time. Her kinky hair was loose and flowed in haphazard curls around her face, giving her an edge. She looked slightly wild and unobtainable and, man, the combination worked for him. Not because he wanted to conquer her, but because he wanted her to conquer him. He wanted to experience that wild side. He'd tasted it last night, and he was now hooked.

He stepped up to her, seeking to put his lips on hers, but changed his mind at the last second. There was a tension between them that crackled and pulsed from their sexual interest. He wanted her stalker to see it. If that person was even in the bar.

Instead, he brushed a kiss by her temple. "Let's go have a drink. We'll sit on the same side of the booth and chat, then get out of there. I want to see if anyone comes up to you."

"Why?" She crossed her arms. Her skin was bumpy with gooseflesh.

"As I figure, if the person was hired, they'll be curious about you. I'm also not ruling out jealousy."

"I haven't dated anyone. My last *anything* was Brad." The way she emphasized anything let him know Brad was the man who'd been before him. Shane's Neanderthal stuck out his head as he envisioned thumping Brad into the ground with his club.

"Maybe someone tried to ask you out and were rebuffed?" He took her hand and led her to the bar.

"I can't think of anyone."

Shane opened the door and, without letting go of her hand, followed Ellie in. To an outsider, his move would look possessive, which was the message he wanted to send. Howlers, the local bar, had seen better days. The place looked worn out. A variety of antlers—pronghorn, elk, and deer—hung high on the wall. Intermittently spaced between them were game heads of the same breeds. Shane wasn't sure any of them were real except maybe the deer. The fur on the heads was shaded lighter from the heavy layer of dust that coated the animals. A neon light hanging over the bar once proclaimed "cold beer" but now said "old beer." Shane wondered if there wasn't some truth to it.

They found a booth so Shane could face the small crowd. He angled his body toward hers but did a quick scan of the group. Mostly local ranch hands. Ellie and Shane were halfway through their drinks with no sign of any attention other than from the waitress when Norris Landry shuffled over. He slid into the bench opposite them.

"It's good to see you out, Ellie," Landry said. "You work too hard."

"We all do," Ellie said.

"True. But I suppose I still see you as that little girl with pigtails. You'd come for a visit every summer with your mom and dad. Now all you do is run from one spot to the next. It'd be nice if you slowed down."

Ellie smiled. "Seems like that was forever ago. Those summer visits, I used to count the days until they came around." She looked at Shane. "You're right. I did need to get out and relax."

"You enjoy yourself tonight, Ellie. Next time you talk to your dad, you tell him I said hi." Landry slid from the booth. He raised his drink in a salute and shuffled away.

"Remind me again about his relationship with you all?" Shane asked.

"According to Grams, dad and Norris Landry were inseparable growing up. The only thing that did eventually separate them was when Dad went off to med school and Landry graduated. He did a degree in geology or something that only required four years. So he returned home while Dad finished med school and his residency. Once Dad graduated, he never returned here, only for visits. But our family always visited the Landrys when we came home."

"And you go to them for help now?" Shane glanced at Norris Landry. The man was the same age as his father but wasn't running the family ranch; he was second in command. Shane imagined such a setup might be demoralizing, assuming Landry wanted to run the ranch. Shane conceded his assumption was broad and based on how Shane would feel. But Shane didn't know many ranchers who weren't ready to be at the helm. Maybe he was wrong, and Norris wasn't a rancher at heart. Maybe the elder Mr. Landry's health was failing and Norris was simply being a good son and staying on. Maybe Norris was more patient than Shane thought. There were too many unknowns, and guesses were just that.

"My grandfather and the older Mr. Landry were good friends. They always helped each other out. Its just something that's always happened." Ellie shrugged and pushed away her empty beer.

"Did Norris ever work in his field?" Shane wondered.

Ellie shrugged. "Maybe. I think at one time he worked for some big oil company or something. But he's always been here since I can remember."

Shane took her hand. "Come on, I want to show you something." He tossed down a tip then tugged her out of the booth.

With a wave to Norris, they left the building. Ellie put up a small fuss, questioning where they were going, but he got her into his truck and drove north of town, beyond the elementary and high school, to Trapper's Stream. A narrow but fast flowing waterway that cut through Wolf Creek and fed into Wind River. The fire hadn't reached this part of town, and the grass was lush and green, the trees budding for spring.

Shane pulled alongside the boat ramp and parked. Dusk was about to give way to night, but the area was lit by the full moon bouncing off the water. Shane took the bag of food. "Follow me." After getting out of the truck he went to her side and opened her door. "I have dessert."

He led her to the tree. "This here's a special tree." Shane set the bag of food to the side.

Ellie walked around it. "What makes it so special?" It was large and so round Shane couldn't wrap his arms around it. The tree's leaves were slowly coming in, and in summer they would offer not only the trunk shade but act as a large umbrella, providing a place to lounge away from the hot sun.

"Its probably only special to me because of this." Shane patted the tree, the spot obscured from the moonbeams. "The roots have grown up and created a seat of sorts. Look." Shane shone his flashlight on the space. The small shelf, the width of three large hands, had been smoothed with time.

"When I was a kid, I would come here and watch the boats come in and out. It was far enough away from the ranch to give me room to think." Shane gestured for her to take a seat.

Ellie wiggled onto the space and leaned back, resting against the trunk. "Its surprisingly comfortable." She looked toward the river. "I imagine the view is very nice during the day because it's pretty cool tonight with the moonlight casting off the river."

Shane leaned his shoulder against the tree so he could see her and the water. "When I got older, I used to think about coming here and having sex. The little seat is perfect. The tree gives enough shade to block a little but its still outdoors, and the thrill of getting caught is there."

Ellie turned to him. "So did you?"

"Have sex here or get caught?"

"Either. Both."

Shane shook his head. "Never dated a girl who was adventurous enough or tall enough."

Ellie chuckled. "Is this you propositioning me?"

"I'll beg if you want." He picked up a ringlet of her hair and twirled it around his finger. "I've been thinking about last night all day today. I want you something fierce, and seeing that skirt makes me even crazier for you."

Ellie pushed at his chest, slightly knocking him back. "Get out of here."

Shane laughed and righted himself. "You ever had sex outside?"

"Does a tent in Africa count?" she said with sass.

"Only half points for that. You were in a tent." Shane moved to stand before her, coming between her knees. "We can go at any time. Just say the word."

"I kinda want to hear you beg," she said and readjusted so all the right parts lined up. The shelf had a slight backward tilt that angled her pelvis just right for him.

"Please, Ellie, make a boyhood dream come true and let's have sex here. Pretty please." He dipped his head, then raked his lips across her neck.

"That's all you got?" She angled her head to give him better access.

"It's an opportunity we'll probably never get again." He kissed the valley between her breasts.

"What's happening here, Shane?" Ellie asked. "Between us. We both know it can't go the distance. Neither of us are looking for long-term. While sleeping with you last night"—she moaned when his hands cupped her breasts—"was amazing, it was foolish. Doing it again would be repeating a mistake."

He lifted his head to look at her, his thumbs still stroking her nipples through the tank top. "This isn't a mistake. We both want it. Hell, we both need it. I say we just enjoy it. Take it for what its worth."

They stared at each other. He couldn't read her expression in the dim light.

She said, "That's the dumbest argument for casual sex I've ever heard."

"Heard a few have you?" He kneaded a little harder and she pushed against him.

"Well, I do watch TV," she said breathlessly.

"Ellie, I'm not going to hurt you. I want to help you stop whoever is doing this to you. I want your farm to succeed. I want you to be happy, and I desperately want to be inside you and feel you wrap yourself around me." He slid his hands down her ribs to her thighs where he gathered up her skirt. He slid his hands up her smooth skin along her legs.

Ellie sagged against the tree. Her hands resting on his shoulders trembled. He slid one hand under the elastic of her panties. Then he slid two fingers inside her. She was hot, wet, and pulsing. He caressed with ease. She began to pant, her fingers digging into his shoulders. He stroked with a rhythm, his thumb rubbing her bud.

He tugged at her panties. "These are in the way," he murmured as he kissed under her ear. She arched up off the ledge, and he made quick work of pulling her panties off. She'd kicked off her boots so the tiny garment slid right off. He traced the path back up to her sweet spot. He was insatiable for her.

Ellie was so uninhibited and vocal that Shane could easily read her. Figuring out what she liked and didn't was simple if he paid attention, and he was an astute student. She fumbled with his belt and jeans, trying to get to his cock.

"Not yet," he told her, his lips brushing kisses along her throat. He massaged in and out with his fingers, teasing her tip.

"I'm going to—" She moaned and quivered, bowing against him.

"I know," he said, holding her close, his face buried in her neck as he moved her closer to ecstasy. She was tense and loose at the same time. He could feel the pressure rising inside her. Her thighs clasped around him tightly.

"Babe, in my pocket is a condom. I need you to put it on me." He leaned back to give her space but continued his stroking.

She grasped at his shoulders like a drowning woman. "I can't think...."

He slowed his stokes.

She grunted in frustration.

"Condom," he reminded her.

She quickly placed the rubber onto his tip and then teased him by slowly rolling it down his length. In retaliation, he began to stroke her quicker. She thrust herself on his fingers. He added another for good measure. She thrust again, and Shane's control slipped. He worked her hard and fast, nipping at her neck. She arched and clenched his fingers hard as she came. He pulled free quickly and watched her writhe as she orgasmed but not arc over.

She pounded a fist on his shoulder. He put his thumb to her pulsing bud and stroked again, softly at first, then with force matching her crescendo. When she became taut, ready to peak, he thrust into her, pumping steadily as she spasmed and gripped him. She trembled in his arms. He was overwhelmed by both the sensations.

"Shane," she screamed as she peaked. "More. Oh, please, give me more."

She surfed the orgasm like a wave and just as she climaxed over the side, he wrapped his arms tighter around her, shifting her so she was coming down on him. He thrust deeper, and her orgasm peaked again.

He'd found that elusive magic spot men live their entire lives thinking about. It left him in awe. Not because he was some sort of male hero but because Ellie had given herself so freely to him, opening herself up fully and taking in everything he had.

It was humbling and an adrenaline rush of the highest form.

He thrust one more time. Hitting the spot. She screamed as pleasure burned her inside and out.

And then he came, too, calling her name. Needing her more than than he'd ever needed anyone or anything.

TUESDAY

Sweet mother of all that was good and holy. Shane Hannigan needed to figure out who was causing her all this grief and get on his way or something bad was going to happen. Like Ellie not wanting him to leave.

This morning she caught herself daydreaming about them doing more things together. Things other than sex. Things like swimming in the river, sex, going camping, sex, and asking his advice on farm issues. She was picturing him in her future, and she simply couldn't have that. Shane was like her dad in that he needed an adventure. He wouldn't be happy here, and Ellie wouldn't be happy anywhere else but here. There was no future for them.

After the mind-blowing sex at the tree—for which she blamed her current irrational fantasies on since no one could sustain that much pleasure and not lose brain cells—Ellie knew she could get used to this, to him. To having him around. Admitting that terrified her to the deepest parts of her being. Other than Grams, she'd been very content to not have anyone else depend upon her, animals excluded. If the farm didn't make vegetables, others understood that the likely cause was Mother Nature. *Being depended on* she could handle. *Being dependent on,* not so much.

Ellie was working the farm stand, getting ready to shut it down for the day, when she noticed a truck parked across the highway, catty-corner from the farm stand. It was like any other ranch or farm truck, a little worse for wear. The body was two-tone, light blue and white. The windows were tinted, and though Ellie couldn't see anyone inside the cab, she had the sense she was being watched. She had noticed the truck earlier when there'd been a handful of customers getting produce and assumed the vehicle belonged to one of them. Only all the customers were gone yet the truck remained. Ellie scolded herself for not paying better attention. Her stomach tumbled with unease, and then a heavy weight of fear settled hard at the bottom. The truck wasn't one she recognized.

Ellie finished with boxing the tomatoes and moved to the peppers, packing what was left. From where she stood, she had an angled view of the truck's front. When she bent over to place veggies in the box, she slid out her phone, slowly bringing it to her side, then swiped her thumb to engage the camera. As covertly as she could, she took pictures, zooming to try to catch the license plate, all while acting like she was packing up the stand. Her hands trembled as she fumbled with both the peppers and the phone.

Ellie glanced over her shoulder behind the farm stand to her parked truck. She instantly saw a problem. The strange truck was parked so the person inside could watch her regardless of where she was positioned, out front or out back. She wanted to call Shane but was afraid. Afraid if she did, the person would leave. Or worse, come after her. She wasn't sure her fears were rational, but she was going with her gut. Instinct was good enough to keep Shane alive in a war zone, it would certainly help one mile from her house.

She loaded the boxes into her truck bed before returning to

the front to snap the vinyl sides into place. Her desire to jump in her truck and speed off was strong, almost overpowering. Fight or flight, right? Yeah, well, she was really feeling the flight part something fierce.

Afterward, Ellie spread out the tarps to cover the produce bins. She fumbled with attaching them to the corners, her nerves twitchy, her attention not on the task. Watching the truck out of the corner of her eye, Ellie gave the farm stand one last inspection to make sure she'd done everything. She jumped when the other truck's engine turned over. Ellie hotfooted it to her truck, locking herself inside as soon as the door slammed shut.

The truck revved its engine, and Ellie glanced in her rearview. The truck had rolled forward so it had a clear view of her and she of it. She pressed Shane's name in her speed dial and put the call on speaker. She set the phone on her lap.

"Hey," he said, "I'm headed your way. Just dropped Joe off at the ranch. Another useless hunt––"

"There's a strange truck behind me." Words tumbled out of her in a rush. "I can't see who it is, but they've been sitting outside the farm stand watching me close it down. I'm afraid to go home because Grams is there." All she had to do was slam her foot to the gas pedal and speed forward down the drive to the farmhouse. But if this person, whoever they may be, wanted to hurt her, she wouldn't lead them to Grams.

"Okay, where are you?" Shane's voice was calm and steady.

Ellie took in her first deep breath. "I'm in my truck. Behind the stand."

The truck revved again.

Her mind raced at the possibilities. Was it going to ram into hers as soon as she got moving? Plow her down the first chance they got? She didn't watch crime dramas on TV, and she didn't read mysteries, but she knew the possibilities of what could happen were endless, and her imagination likely wasn't capable of creating the worst scenario. As a kid, with her parents, her biggest fears were wildlife, predators such as lions. Or big-ass scary spiders. She never imagined this.

"I'm about ten minutes from you. Stay calm. Can you head toward town. We'll cross paths."

"I suppose." When Ellie shifted into reverse, the truck pulled in behind her, blocking her. Her heart skipped a beat and sweat broke out on her brow. Ellie sucked in a quivering breath. Her voice several octaves higher, she told Shane, "I can't back up. He's blocking me."

"Can you go forward and then cut across the grass?"

She was impressed with how calm he sounded.

"Look at all the alternatives, Ell. Not just forward and back. Don't get out of the truck."

Ellie took a deep breath, fighting for control, and looked in her rearview mirror. "It's a guy. I can't tell who. He's got his hat pulled down low, but it's a dark hat. Stetson." Ellie scanned the space around her. If she went forward and to the left, around the farm stand, there was a ditch she could get stuck in. But also, truck guy could block her from heading to town, forcing her to drive away from both the house and Shane. If she went right, then he could T-bone her and what then?

"Shane, I'm scared. I want to run but nowhere seems safe. I don't want him to follow me home," she wailed.

The truck moved forward and bumped into her.

"He's pushing me," she cried. "Trying to push me forward maybe?" She pressed her foot on the brake. Her truck was in park but nudged forward slightly. Truck guy revved his engine.

"Stay calm. I know its hard because its scary, but he'll get ahead of you if you panic."

A trickle of tears ran down her face. "Easy for you to say."

"I want you to put it into drive and pull forward slightly like you're reeling in a fish. Nice and slow. When you've played with him a bit, say when his truck gets to where your truck is now, I want you to floor it and turn left. Like jerking the line. Got it?"

"Yeah, then what?" She put a shaky hand on the gear shifter.

"Then I want you to come in behind him. Do what he's doing to you. He'll likely back up and try to cut you off. I want you to turn into him," Shane said firmly.

"Why would I do that?" She lifted her hand off the shifter, uncertain if she could do as Shane asked. Or if she even wanted to.

"You have to get control of this situation. He wants to chase you. Do not run," he said, the last words with great emphasis. "You can do this, Ell. I'm almost there, but you cannot wait for me."

He was right. What if he hadn't been around? What would she have done then? Ellie put the truck into drive and inched forward. The truck stayed on her bumper. She went forward an inch, he pushed her forward another. It was a tedious process and felt like it took eons when she knew it had only been seconds. When she was a good foot beyond the farm stand Ellie closed her eyes, said a brief prayer for courage, then as she held her breath she slammed down the gas. Briefly, her truck spun on the gravel road before getting purchase and fishtailed as it lurched forward. She grabbed the wheel with both hands and jerked it to the left, correcting quickly so as to not hit the farm stand. In a cloud of dust and grass, she sped across the land and onto the road. She righted the truck and pointed it to town.

Shane's words echoed in her head. *Do. Not. Run.*

But the urge was too great, and the opening was there. Truck guy had followed her forward instead of backing up, and she wasn't going to drive home anyway. Truck guy's actions hadn't been in the plan.

"What's happening?" Shane asked.

"He followed me. I'm headed toward you now," Ellie cried, leaning forward in her seat. It was then she realized she hadn't put her seatbelt on. Too distracted by the truck guy. She tried to reach for it, but her speed made her uncomfortable, and she put her hand back on the wheel.

"No, Ellie. You need to slow down. Don't let him chase you. Slow down and stop right there in the road. I'm minutes away," Shane shouted.

Truck guy sped up, and she could see him coming in fast. He swerved to her left, and she understood then why Shane had told her not to run. But it was too late. She slammed on the brakes, tires squealing on the pavement as her truck shuddered and skid down the road. Truck guy, apparently not anticipating her action, swerved into her but his rear bumper caught her left front panel, causing her to spin to the right. Ellie screamed. Her backend fish-tailed, spun another ninety degrees before sliding into the ditch, bouncing hard, facing in the opposite direction.

"Ellie," Shane yelled, his voice adding to the chaos of noise filling her space.

Without the security of her seatbelt, Ellie bounced just as hard as the truck and slammed into the driver's door, her head banging against the glass, causing a starburst of light to cloud her vision. Velocity pushed her forward, her head connected with the steering wheel, and everything went black.

17

TUESDAY

S hane passed the blue and white truck as it sped past him, and every part of him wanted to turn his vehicle around and chase the man down. Only the echoing sounds of Ellie's scream had kept him focused on her. If she was hurt... He was unable to finish the thought.

She was regaining consciousness when he ran up to the truck. Thankfully, the damage to her and the vehicle weren't terrible. But there shouldn't be *any* damage. This shouldn't have happened.

Shane made her wait in the truck until the ambulance and then allowed them to move her. She was alert and responsive, and though she now sat on the side of the ambulance answering the medic's questions, still it did not put Shane at ease. His fury barely restrained, he was wound so tight the slightest provocation would unleash a beat-down of epic proportions. He wanted to find this guy something awful. Never in his life had he wanted anything more than to right this wrong. He was desperate for it. Could feel the need of doing so surging inside him. He was in an unhealthy place; the time wasn't right for him to go primal. He uncurled his fist, blew out a deep breath, and focused on Ellie.

"You should go to the hospital like he wants," Shane repeated. Ellie was being as stubborn as one of her goats.

"So they can tell me I have a concussion? I already know I do." She held still while the paramedic put butterfly stitches across the gash in her forehead.

"You're lucky you don't need this sewn up," said Wyatt, the paramedic, also one of the town's fireman.

"Yes, lucky. That's me," Ellie replied.

Wyatt turned to Shane. "Just watch her through the night. If she stops breathing, complains of her headache getting worse, or starts vomiting then take her in. No exceptions."

Shane nodded and focused on Ellie. "I called Carl to come get your truck."

Fort had arrived minutes after Shane, who'd called him as soon as he'd reached Ellie's truck. The sheriff was all business as he stood next to the ambulance in his uniform with a small note-book in his hand.

"I have an APB out for this truck. As soon as you can, I'll need you to send me those photos you have," Fort said.

"If I'm so lucky, then maybe I caught the license," Ellie said as she took Wyatt's hand. He then helped her out of the ambulance.

"I sure hope so, " Fort said. "I'll come by when I get off and make sure you're doing okay. If I know anything sooner than that, I'll call."

Ellie swayed where she stood.

"We'll be at the farm. You can always call my number, too." Wrapping an arm around her, Shane helped her to his truck.

"I can walk," she said leaning heavily against him.

"I know." He kissed the top of her head, his heartrate finally slowing down.

"I'm sorry I didn't listen to you. I panicked."

"It happens. Its not like you do this sort of thing often. I'm just glad you're okay." When they reached the truck, he lifted her into the seat then reached across to get the seatbelt.

They drove back to the farm in silence, Ellie with her head against the headrest, eyes closed. When they pulled up outside the house, she said, "Play it down for Grams, will ya? Just say I got into an accident or something."

"You know I can't do that. It might work for now, but soon people will be calling to ask about you. I'm sure someone heard it on the police scanner." He handed over her phone. He'd found it behind the cab's bench seat. It was a miracle it hadn't broke. "Can you get those photos out to Fort now? Sooner is better than later."

Ellie used her thumb to open the phone and handed it to Shane. "Can you?"

He sent what he could. From his quick scan, it looked like Ellie had managed to capture the last two numbers of the plate.

Grams came out on the porch with her arms crossed, a worried expression on her face.

"Time to face the music," Shane said.

Ellie groaned. He helped her up the stairs.

Grams, looking pale, shook her head. "This has got to stop. What do they want?"

Shane met her gaze and shrugged. If he knew, then he could make it stop. Until then, he wanted nothing more than to tuck Ellie and Grams away at his parents' ranch to keep them safe. Confrontations were hard for Ellie. She preferred to avoid them. He preferred to deal with them head on and be done with it. Regardless, Ellie needed to accept a big confrontation was coming. One she couldn't avoid. He could smell its impending arrival on the wind, and she would hold steady for its arrival. He knew better than to ask her to hide out at his parents'. Her rejection of the idea would be swift and firm. Oh, how he wished she'd run.

He now understood what his parents must have felt knowing he was in constant danger. Or when Laura had died. How people were connected was moot. Family, friend, it didn't matter. Caring for someone who was in harms way was a difficult burden to carry every day. Caring for someone who was unexpectedly hurt or a victim of a tragedy was a punch to the heart. When he'd seen Ellie's truck, he'd only thought of her and her safety. When he knew she was going to be okay, he'd thought of his sister and the car accident that had taken her life. Death could happen in a snap. He should know. He'd brought death to others in mere second from a trigger pull.

The events of the day were cutting too close to home. Now, he no longer begrudged his mother her look of relief when he'd told her he might be an instructor at sniper school. He now understood the diminished spark in the eyes of Laura's widower, Deke.

"Let's get you on the couch to rest," Shane said hoarsely.

Once Ellie was settled, a blanket tucked around her, two pillows under her head, a glass of iced tea in reach, Shane took a moment in the kitchen alone to gather his thoughts.

Maybe Ellie was on to something with running away from entanglements. Sometimes the threads that connected cut deep.

Her phone rang, and Shane went into the living room to see if it was Fort.

"It's my dad," Ellie said and groaned.

"If you don't take it, he'll only keep calling," Grams warned and shuffled away.

She sighed and accepted the call. He tried not to listen and, truthfully, she didn't say much. He stepped into the kitchen to give her privacy but sat at the chair closest to the doorway. Eavesdropping meant information was how he justified it. Only the conversation was mostly boring. A whole lot of "I'm okay" and "No, I'm not moving back there, wherever there is this month."

Shane knew she was taking a verbal beating. He'd been on the end of that kind of tirade before. Typically, from his mother. His ears perked up when he heard her mention her ex-fiancé.

"Dad, I don't care what you tell Brad. Tell him someone ran me off the road. Don't tell him. Frankly, I don't think it's any of his business."

Shane wished he could hear the other half of the conversation. He was proud of Ellie for holding her own.

Ellie snorted, and Shane leaned closer to the door. He noticed Grams was eavesdropping from the foyer. She gave him a wink.

She grunted her irritation. "How lucky for Brad that he's on a supply run," she said sarcastically. "No, Dad. I do not care that people get out of the country more than before. I don't want to be 'in country'. Not even for a day, and offering me the job of doing the supply runs so I can 'get away' as you just called it does not appeal to me whatsoever."

He heard another grunt, this one muffled and looked around the corner. Ellie was banging the phone against the couch arm.

"Are you done talking?" she asked when she put it back to her ear. She closed her eyes and her head fell back against the stacked pillows. "No, I wasn't listening, but then neither are you. Listen, Dad, I have a terrible headache. I would like to get some rest. Can we do this some other time?"

She sighed heavily. "Yeah, sure. I love you, too." She ended the call and tossed the phone to the foot of the couch.

"You can come in Grams. I know you're out there listening," Ellie called.

Grams shuffled in. Shane stood in the doorway separating the family room and the kitchen.

Ellie pressed fingers to her temples. "Well, Grams, looks like Dad knows you and I can't do this farm thing. We should just give it up. You should move to Florida, and I should just go wherever they go." She pressed a hand to her head. "I wish he would hear me for once when I say I don't want do what they do. You know how clueless he is? He even tried to guilt me by using Brad. Said he wasn't going to tell Brad and cause him needless worry since I'm okay and all."

"I don't want to live in Florida. What am I supposed to do there? Play shuffleboard all day long?" Grams plopped into her recliner and picked up her knitting needles. Following a shake of her head, she said, "But maybe he's right..."

Ellie sat up with a start and groaned loudly as a result. Shane considered leaving them to have this private talk, but he wasn't sure how to extricate himself from the room.

"Maybe we aren't doing such a good job of running this farm. It gets harder every day." Her needles clanked, marking her frustration.

"We were going fine, Grams, until this nonsense happened. Yeah, at times things were a little tight, but we were making it. We're still making it."

"Barely. Where's the money gonna come from to fix your truck?" Grams asked.

"Insurance." Ellie wagged an angry finger in the air. "And when I find out who this butthead is that did this to me, I'm gonna sue him."

"How are you gonna pay for a lawyer? Hmm? We can't even afford to fix the irrigation system. Today I found a hose cut."

Shane straightened. Ellie slumped back in defeat.

"Which hose?" Shane asked.

"The one farthest away from the house. She pointed to the crops outside the back of the house.

Ellie pressed her palms to her eyes. "I don't want to let whoever is doing this win," she said.

Grams needles stilled. "Neither do I, honey, but I also don't want to lose you, and today really scared me."

Ellie nodded. "I'm sorry, Grams."

"It's not your fault, honey." Grams went back to her project.

"I'm going to go out and take a look at the hoses," Shane said and stood.

"Before you go, there's one more thing," Grams said and pointed to a folded packet of papers on the TV stand.

Ellie groaned. "I can't wait to hear this."

"See that packet. Grab it for me, will you Shane?"

He did as she asked and held it out to her. She shook her head.

"Go ahead and read it. Might as well read it out loud so Ellie can hear, too,"

When Shane unfolded the papers, the state seal in the corner caught his eye. It was from the county tax assessor. He scanned the top page. His unresolved anger from the accident was rising quickly, ready to spill out. He clenched his jaw from swearing up a streak.

"What is it?" Ellie asked, her voice rigid and faint.

"My guess is someone reported you to the tax assessor."

"For what? We're paid up." She swung her legs off the couch, intending to get up. Shane went and sat next to her.

"Someone brought to the tax assessor's attention an old tax code. One that cites if a landowner has so many animals on the land that aren't domestic, meaning used for products, they can be reclassified as a ranch." Shane looked at the next page. It was a tax bill. For over seven thousand dollars. He whistled.

"I don't get it," Ellie said and reached for the papers. He handed her the top page.

"Because of the goats and llama, the farm is now classified as a ranch, and because of that, you owe taxes. It looks like they are going back two years. How long have you had the goats?"

"Not two years," Ellie mumbled as she scanned the page. "This is bullcrap."

"Well, you can fight it. It's gonna cost you a lot of time and maybe a lawyer." He handed her the tax bill.

Ellie gasped, her eyes becoming glassy with tears. "Someone hates us."

"It would seem that way," Grams said.

"Actually, Grams, someone hates me. Maybe if I left, then all this would go away." Ellie looked between Shane and her grandmother.

"Then I would have to sell. Call me a crazy old woman, but I'd always envisioned leaving this farm to family." Grams shook her head. "It made me so happy you found your home here, that you love this place as much as I do, but maybe your father is right." Grams stopped knitting and dropped her yarn and needles in the basket beside her chair. "I wish we could figure this thing out." She pushed out of the chair and shuffled out of the room.

"I'll get rid of the goats and the llama," Ellie said.

"They make you money, don't they?" Shane reasoned.

Ellie fell back against the couch, tears running down her face. "I don't know what to do, Shane."

He nodded. "Let's not do anything yet. Let me read the rest of this. I also want to call my dad. But first I'm going to check the hoses, and you're going to get some rest."

He forced her to lie back down and once again tucked the blanket around her. "This doesn't have to be addressed today or even tomorrow. We have time."

"How much time?" she mumbled.

"More than you think." He took the paper from her and set it out of arm's reach. If she saw ninety days with accruing interest, she'd lose her mind and all ability for reason.

He found Grams in the kitchen. She poured him a mug of coffee then sat at the table. She gestured for him to do the same. She ran a finger over a cut in the butcher-block tabletop, sighed, then looked out the window. "My parents started this farm. Built it from the ground up. This house used to be four rooms. They built that up as well. Always planning to add on." Her voice caught.

"You can't tell they added on," Shane said.

"Earl and I added the second floor. We spent extra money to make sure the house would look like a proper farmhouse and not some hodgepodge Lego pieces house." Grams chuckled at her own joke. "We've had some hard times before, that's for sure. Droughts, fires, seed gone bad. But something we learned early on was farms and ranches that carried large debts never made it. Too top heavy. We promised each other we'd never do that. Never take money out against the farm." She tapped the center of her chest. "Always felt wrong right here, know what I mean."

"Yes ma'am, I do. My parents have the same philosophy." He knew other ranches and farmers who didn't. Shane had considered hardship of another ranch or farm as motive but couldn't figure out what anyone would gain by taking the Greenes' farm. They weren't sitting on any oil or anything like that.

"We got lucky a few times. Ellie ever tell you about the sapphire her grandfather found?"

Shane nodded. He knew the foothills were scattered with all types of rocks, gems, and minerals. But there weren't riches to be found out there, no one expected to find piles of gold or sapphire. Only the odd gem here and there and mostly due to the odd strike of good luck. A person had a better chance at winning by playing the lottery.

"That sapphire carried us through some hard times. Too bad we don't have one now." Grams dismissed her musings with a breezy wave. "I'm telling you all this because Ellie knows this farm's history. She's not going to take a loan out on the farm. She won't be the generation to put us in debt." Grams pressed her lips together tightly, her eyes watering. "I think its time to sell. You're gonna have to help me convince her to do it."

Shane shook his head. "Let's not go there yet. We haven't exhausted all options."

"But the time will come—"

Shane put his hand over hers. "And when it does, we can have that conversation."

Grams nodded and patted her other hand over his. "You're a good one, Shane. Like your dad."

Before Shane could answer, his phone rang. The screen showed Fort's name.

"Tell me you caught him," Shane said.

Then he listened, tensing at what he heard. .

18

WEDNESDAY

"**G**et married? Are you nuts? That's the most...asinine idea I have ever heard," Ellie said to the crowd.

No one would make eye contact with her. Shane sat next to her on the couch where he'd forced her to spend the afternoon "recuperating." She'd been able to get through her daily schedule but not without him dogging her every step. The minute she'd finished the last of the farm chores, two-thirds of them he'd done in the time it'd taken her to do her portion, he'd whisked her up in his arms, marched into the house, and planted her on the couch with strict orders to not move.

She hadn't. She'd napped next to Benny for a bit, did some hand sewing on Cori's baby blanket, and now sat across from her friends, lunatics the lot of them, and listened to their idea. She was glad Grams was having dinner at the diner with her knitting friends. Ellie wasn't sure if Grams would be as stunned by the idea of marriage as Ellie was or approve of it. Ellie wasn't sure she wanted to know.

Deke Sutton, the state's assistant insurance commissioner, had also shown up. Apparently Fort had invited him because of his connection with the tax assessor. And by connection, Deke's office was across the hall from the assessors. Deke was Shane and Cricket's brother in law, though he'd been a widower over seven years now.

They'd shown up with fixings for lasagna and a few six packs of hand-crafted beers, each of them ready to find a solution to Ellie's problems. It was the last one, proposed by Sabrina, that was the most ludicrous. Marriage! As if that made any sense.

"I don't even understand how that will make a difference. I'll still owe the taxes." Ellie shook her head in disbelief. She leaned back against the couch and pulled the afghan up to her waist. Shane got up and started a fire. Evening was turning into night, and the cool mountain air was sweeping across the farm, bringing with it a chill.

Hannah turned her laptop to face Ellie. "That's not true, actually. You already know the tax law is older than dirt. Came into play after the civil war. From what I've found, the purpose of the tax law was to help widows save their farms and ranches. So if they married a rancher or farmer who was current with their taxes, then the penalty was absorbed, for the most part."

Ellie chuffed. "By letting someone else take over for them?"

Hannah shrugged. "Remember. Women weren't even allowed to vote then. But think of it this way—a woman loses her husband, she gets the property. If the property struggles or if she gets hit with the tax because she's trying to be prosperous and grow, much like you're attempting to do, then who would want to take on that mess? And getting married allows the woman to keep her property and doesn't penalize the man by making him take on the tax fee."

"So the bill just goes away?" Cori asked.

"Not entirely. There is a small fee. Five percent of the tax bill still needs to be paid."

"It does sound very misogynistic," Cricket said. She glared at Deke.

"Why are you looking at me like this is my fault? I didn't write the bill," Deke exclaimed.

"No, but bureaucrats like you did." Cricket crossed her arms and looked away.

Ellie studied them. There was a weird dynamic between Cricket and Deke. Ellie couldn't put her finger on it. The irritation Cricket projected toward Deke didn't seem like it was because he annoyed her. On the contrary, the way Cricket kept stealing furtive glances at him indicated Cricket was distracted by Deke's presence. Occasionally, Ellie caught an expression on Cricket's face Ellie thought might be longing. Ellie wondered if Cricket's feelings ran more along the way of interest. Ellie wondered what that was like, being interested in her deceased sister's husband. Dealing with her feelings for Shane were hard enough knowing he was leaving, but had he belonged to someone she loved first... Ellie shook her head. She couldn't imagine it. She studied Cricket; the more she watched the clearer it was. Cricket had a thing for Deke. Ellie's heart went out to the woman.

"Why are you even here, Deke?" Cricket asked.

Deke's shoulders slumped, and he sighed wearily. He addressed the group. "Fort asked me to come. I talked to the tax assessor, a nice guy by the name of Kyle Petry. He received a call from his boss telling him to check out Ellie's situation. His boss said he was doing it for a friend and wouldn't mention who. Kyle talked to Fort and told him what he knows. By law he's required to check up on all tax evasion type issues."

"I'm not trying to evade taxes," Ellie cried.

Fort leaned forward, resting his elbows on his knees. He tapped his finger on the coffee table. "Let me add this. Whoever drove that truck knew what they were doing. Not only was the truck stolen, but the plates, too. The cab was wiped clean. The person—"

"A guy. I know it was a guy. I could make out that much when I saw him."

Fort shrugged and conceded the point. "The guy even knew not to park by CCTV cameras. We can trace him into Bison's Prairie where he ditched the car, but he was never caught on CCTV. At least, not while ditching the car."

"Could it have been Lester Phillips in the truck?" Shane asked.

Ellie didn't have to give the question thought. The identity of truck guy was all she thought of in her downtime. She tried to picture all her neighbors and friends behind the wheel, hoping her gut would point her in the right direction. Trouble was she had a hard time imagining anyone she knew doing this to her and Grams.

Ellie rubbed her temple. "I don't think so. Mr. Phillips isn't overly tall. This guy was. He had the visor down, his hat low, and all I could see was below his nose.

"Why Phillips?" Deke asked.

"He found gold, believes the boulder could have tumbled down from Ellie's land. Wasn't he hard up after the fires?" Shane asked Deke, who also happened to be the insurance man for many townsfolk.

Deke grimaced and shook his head as if he wasn't certain. "Its hard for me to picture him doing it. I'm assuming he's not hurting for money because he won't buy insurance. Even after the loss he suffered from the fire. Says he doesn't need it. My gut says he's not financially desperate."

"But you're just guessing. Maybe he doesn't get insurance because Phillips is anti-government and against supporting the man. Maybe that's why he doesn't buy insurance. Remember back when we had those cattle rustlers? Even as cattle were being stolen from his herd, he didn't tag and register his cows, which would have given him more protection," Cricket said.

"That's true," said Fort. "But he does tag and register them now. He likes going after crooks more than he dislikes the government. He's grumbled to me once or twice about tagging. Says he does it for me, to help me catch rustlers should we have more. And with meth on the rise in our remote area, it's only a matter of time before we see more rustling."

Deke held up a finger. "Phillips and I did talk during that time. I tried hard to sell him insurance. He showed me a cost-benefit statement to show why he wasn't getting insurance, and I'll admit, based on what he showed me, it was more fiscally sound to not have insurance. His losses were minimal."

"Until the fire," added Fort.

"But then he found gold," Shane said.

"Its a dead end, then?" Ellie asked. Phillips didn't strike her as financially greedy either. He'd always seemed content with living simply.

"For now," Fort answered, "but I'm not walking away from this."

"Damn right, you aren't. None of us are," Shane said. "But we can't deny the stakes have been raised. Whoever did this will probably go further next time. You could be *really* hurt. No more chicken racing. And I think what they want is the farm."

Ellie's gaze met Shane's, and she nodded. "Yeah, I mean, why else cause us financial hardships?"

Sabrina, who'd been standing by the couch, sat on the edge. "Well, there could be other reasons to do that, but those don't look to be in play here."

"Reasons like what?" Ellie asked. She couldn't imagine what Sabrina was talking about.

Shane interrupted. "We should get back to the issue at hand." He caught Ellie's eye and pointed to Cori, who was yawning but trying to cover it.

Ellie considered her friends with children waiting for them at home. Friends with babies on the way. Cricket was the only one in a similar situation to Ellie. No man or kids. Except Cricket owned her own home and had a job. And no one was trying to take that from her.

"So you're telling me I can either pay this bill, sell my goats—"

"You'll still owe the bill if you sell the goats, only a little less since it's projected for the remainder of the year," Deke said.

"Okay, I'll need to sell my goats and llama to pay less of a tax bill with money I don't have. I can be the first Greene to take out a loan on the farm, but with the way things are going, I don't think that's a good option." She faced Shane. "Remember when you told me to trust my gut. My gut says taking out a loan is exactly what this guy wants. I won't compromise the farm any more than I have."

"Do you have anything you can sell?" Cori asked.

"Not enough to make seven thousand dollars." Ellie rapidly blinked, hoping to keep the tears from bursting free. Every time she said the amount out loud, she'd cried. Someone must really hate her to do this, and her life was a sad state of affairs if seven thousand dollars could break her. Shoot, two thousand would break her. Seven would destroy her.

"Getting married is a viable option. I know several couples who've married for similar reasons and have found happiness," Sabrina said and took Ellie's hand. "I know it's a wild concept, to marry to save your ranch. With our modern times, we have all these ideas about one love and being swept off our feet. Not that those aren't wonderful sentiments, but they won't get a couple through the rough times. Times like fires and illness."

"And pregnancy gas," Fort said then coughed in his hand.

His wife jammed her elbow in his ribs. "At least pregnancy farts have a valid reason. What about chili farts and beef jerky farts and—"

Fort cupped his hand over her mouth. "We get the idea."

Ellie nodded toward Fort and Cori and gave Sabrina a pointed look. "Compatibility needs to be there, too," she argued. "And who do I marry? Who would want to marry me for this reason? There are one thousand other problems that come with this."

Cricked coughed. "Ah, Shane's free."

Ellie's attention swung to Shane and found he'd been watching her. She tossed her hand up in frustration. "Did you know you were going to be the sacrificial lamb?"

His expression a mask, she had no idea what he was thinking. "I had an idea. When Hannah told me about the law, Cricket was there. I could see her wheels racing. When you've grown up with someone, they aren't that hard to predict. I wasn't sure she was going to bring it up, though." He turned his attention to Cricket. "What makes you think this is such a good idea?"

Cricket gave a delicate shrug and had the decency to blush. "Well, I mean you're the obvious answer." She slapped her knee in frustration. "Look, it *is* a crazy idea, sure. But it could work. Yeah, it's a marriage of convenience. But there are worse reasons to get married, and no one is saying you have to stay married."

Ellie groaned and stood. She moved to stand by the fireplace, the practicality of the conversation leaving her cold. "What girl wouldn't love to have that on her record? A marriage of convenience and a divorce when it was no longer needed, a disposable marriage. Wow." She rubbed her hands up and down her arms.

"Which appeals to you less? A marriage to me or to Brad?" Shane asked.

"Who's Brad?" Cricket questioned. "Could he be behind this?"

Ellie waved off her question. "He lives in Africa, so it's not him. I'm sorry, I don't understand the leap to marriage. Can't I make payment plans? There has to be something like that available."

Hannah nodded. "Sure, there is. The interest rate is very high and the farm is collateral. You'd be better off with a bank loan."

"Why am I the only one here who thinks this idea is so far out of this world it's almost inconceivable? I can't wrap my head around it and yet, here we are, talking about it like its an option. Why would Shane agree to such a thing? What does he get out of it?" Ellie pointed out.

She looked around the room. "Fort, do you think this is a good idea?"

Fort looked contrite. "Ell, truth is, I hired Cori to pretend to be my girlfriend so I could win an election. I might not be the person to ask."

Cori giggled. "Look at us now."

Ellie moved on. "Bryce?"

Bryce was sitting on the floor next to Hannah who was in Grams recliner. He clasped his hands, resting them on his knee. "Its not for me to say. I've seen stranger things work out. And as for what Shane gets out of it, well, that's for him to say."

Ellie faced Shane, who gave her a wry smile.

"Why don't you and I talk about this after everyone leaves. The options are on the table, and we can go over them again. It's been a long day, cute-face, and this is a lot to think about." His face softened. "I think you should go to bed."

Ellie felt heat rush through her body. When she thought of bed, she thought of Shane naked. She met his gaze and knew he was thinking the same thing. Of her naked, not himself. She cracked a smile. "Okay," she said softly, nodding.

"Well," Cricket said, jumping to her feet. "I don't know about you all, but I think that's our cue to leave. Things just got warm in here." The others got up and started gathering their jackets and purses.

Ellie groaned from embarrassment. She struggled to say something that would convince them she and Shane weren't going to have sex when everyone was gone.

Shane moved to stand beside her. "Don't bother," he said in her ear then laughed. "They won't believe you, and why lie?"

Sabrina came over. "I'm ordained. You could get a license tomorrow and be married that fast." Sabrina snapped her fingers. "This bill would be gone."

Ellie nodded, but she found the knowledge that tomorrow she could be hitched scary. Things were happening too fast. Sabrina squeezed her shoulder then turned to leave.

"I'll drive you home, Cricket," Ellie heard Deke say.

"You wish," Cricket retorted.

"Don't be ridiculous," Deke said as the group shuffled down the hall to the front door. "Who did you come here with?"

Cricket stomped her foot. "Fine. You can take me."

Shane chuckled again. "She rode with me. I'm going get to the bottom of what's going on between Cricket and Deke before I leave," he said. "But it can wait. I need to get you to bed."

Ellie gulped. She couldn't wait.

19

WEDNESDAY

Sex with Shane should be called something more. Something that sounded grand and stunning. Because sex with him was both those things and so much more. In light of her bruises and achy body parts, Shane handled her with a gentleness she'd never experienced. Maybe as a baby perhaps when her mother had been new and uncertain. Shane had folded her in his arms and, while staring into her eyes, had kept his rhythm easy like a soft caress, a seductive dance. In no time, he'd gently swayed her over the edge and floated her to the ground. In his arms, she let go of all her worries and lived in the moment. If she could stitch these moments into a quilt, she'd be able to cover herself with them and feel their warmth for the rest of her life. Long after he'd return to the Marines. These moments were glorious, magical, and healing. They gave her strength.

Ellie laid across him, her cheek on his chest, his hand stroking the back of her head, his fingers occasionally tangling in her hair.

"You think us getting married to save this farm is stupid, right?" She needed to broach the subject. It was a fat elephant in the room.

"Stupid might not be the right word." His chest vibrated from the deep rumbling of his voice.

"I can't reconcile myself to the idea," she whispered.

His hand on her hair stilled. "Of marrying me? It's that foreign of an idea?"

"Of marrying for something other than love. For something as practical as money."

"People do it all the time. Think of trophy wives."

Ellie heaved a deep sigh and pushed up, coming to rest on her forearm. She looked down at him. "I'm the one that gets everything out of this idea. What do you get?"

"Satisfaction from helping you out? Listen, we can solve this problem right now if you let me loan you the money." He ran a hand down her shoulder.

She shook her head. "What if I couldn't pay it back? I couldn't live with myself."

"I have faith in you. I know you'll be able to pay me back. Besides, it would give me great pleasure to win this battle. And yeah, I don't get anything out of the deal, according to you. But I do get satisfaction in knowing I helped. In knowing I stopped this guy—"

"But it's a temporary stop. When you leave—"

"Stop shoving me out the door."

Ellie snorted. She sat up and curled her legs beneath her, wrapping the sheet around her chest. "You have one foot out the door already."

"I'm right here, right now." He took her hand and stroked his chest with it. "Feel that? That's me, right here."

"Maybe physically, but how about mentally? You're still committed to your job, as you should be. My guess is everything here is a distraction until you have your orders, or whatever it is you are waiting on."

Something flickered in his eyes. Ellie couldn't read it, but he looked away, and it was then she knew she'd spoken the truth.

She continued. "Yes or no. The Marines call right now and say you can have your job back. Yes or no?"

"What?" He shook his head in confusion.

"Yes or no, you want to be a sniper. Decide right now, yes or no." She pushed him on the shoulder. "Decide."

"Ellie—"

"Yes or no!" she said with urgency.

"Yes!" he said, sitting up and pushing her away with agitation. His expression hardened. "Yes," he repeated quieter. "I've always wanted to be a sniper. I wasn't ready for it to end when it did. I'm not ready for my military career to end."

A little bubble of hope she'd unknowingly been carrying around with her burst. "What's happening between us is great. Its fun and, truth is, it's what I needed." She gestured between them. "But this is casual. This is temporary. We both want different things, and I think we both knew that going into this."

"Agreed," he said. "Which is why the marriage thing might be a good idea."

Ellie rolled her eyes and flopped down to the bed.

"Listen to me. You're thinking about it from a love standpoint. You need to see it as a business deal."

She pointed a finger at him. "Only you get nothing in the arrangement."

"My last name carries a lot of weight. This maniac of yours would be stupid to keep messing with you. It could get your dad off your back."

Ellie smiled. "Now that's the best argument I've heard yet."

"You're putting yourself in a corner here. You realize that, right?" He lightly tugged at a corkscrew lock, then let it go to bounce around.

"I have to decide on something, I know. I just don't like any of the options." She tossed a hand in the air with frustration. "I mean, get married? That sounds absurd to you too, right?"

Shane tucked his hands under his head and sighed. "The idea of being married would sound more absurd if I lived here full-time because then I'd be trying to make a go of life here to make the marriage feel more real. Does that make sense? If we both lived here, and word got out we weren't living together or anything, then that would look bad. It would spark questions. But if I'm living in Cali because of work and you're here taking care of the farm and Grams, people would understand the separation. Or I think they would. "

Ellie flopped down on the bed beside him. "Why is someone doing this to me?"

Shane blew out a breath. "Listen. There's something you need to know. I didn't want to tell you because I don't want it to influence your decision, but I think you need to know because... Well, you need to know."

Ellie rolled to her side to face him. His flat and serious tone was not giving her any good feels. "Is this going to be another bomb? I'm not sure I can handle anything more."

Shane heaved a heavy sigh then looked at her, his body not moving. "I got an email from my friend back in California earlier today. My med-board will be decided soon. It's still unofficial, but rumor is they're going to keep me. My source is pretty reliable. I'll be returning to duty."

Briefly, Ellie closed her eyes then nodded slowly. "Yeah, of course. This is great news, right? Earlier you said you'd go back in a heartbeat."

"Well, I don't think they'll put me back as a sniper, but I can be an instructor." He looked away, his jaw hardening after he'd said "instructor," as if the word was a demotion.

"That's just as good. Someone had to teach you, and now you can pass that along." She studied him, wondering if he thought of the job in that way. Wondering if he saw that he could make a difference that way and have a hand at creating the next generation of snipers.

"That's a positive way to look at it, I suppose." Shane stared at the ceiling.

Ellie gave a half smile. "Silver linings. They keep me going." She laid back and stared at the ceiling, too. "When you say soon, do you have an idea?"

Shane grunted. She'd come to learn what those grunts meant simply by the length and depth of them. This one told her he wasn't happy about the answer he was about to give. Her stomach clenched.

"No, but my guess is next week. I might have to leave before we get this resolved." He wiped his hand down his face and across the scruff blooming on his chin.

Ellie pressed her palms to her eyes. She didn't want him to see the fear and hurt she was feeling. Yeah, she was scared of what would happen once he left. She'd quickly become attached to his presence around the farm. She was also afraid of what the days would be like when he was gone. Empty, came to mind. Boring. Dull. The throbbing ache of hurt in her chest was the emotion that surprised her the most. Her logical mind had been expecting this. It was her heart that ached now.

"Ellie?" he whispered.

She pressed the palms harder to force any tears that might be thinking of breaking free to turn back. She would not cry.

"Cute-face, look at me."

The bed shifted, and she knew he'd come up on his side and was staring at her.

"I just need a second," she whispered back.

"I'm not going to leave you high and dry."

Ellie sucked in a deep breath and let it out slowly. She moved her palms away. "I know you won't. Only, I'm afraid I can't do this without you." She gave a reticent laugh. "Which is precisely why I didn't want you here in the first place."

"You can do this without me. You were doing it before I came.

And you'll still have me. I can be on the phone and troubleshoot with you all the time. You'll have the others, too."

She faced him and cupped his cheek in her hand. "It won't be the same."

He kissed the inside of her palm. "I know. This is why I'm not opposed to us getting married. I sure would feel a hell of a lot better when I left if I knew you had the Hannigan name to help you."

"Its a temporary fix." She caressed his cheek once more before letting her hand fall to the bed.

"Yeah, but that might be all we need. Once we get to the bottom of this, then it will be over. But until then, it will still be my way of helping. That's what I'm getting out of it." Shane searched her face. He was trying to read her.

"Okay," she whispered. She was tired of looking for the perfect solution. She was tired of not knowing what to do, and she was scared to be without him. She hoped her agreement wasn't some last ditch desperate effort to keep him close.

"Okay? This is the way you want to go? Become the old ball and chain?" His brows shot up, surprised.

"Well, when you put it like that?" she teased. "But a marriage of convenience makes sense, I guess." She pointed her finger at him. "I'm going to tell Grams the truth, and you're going to be there with me."

"Of course," he said. "I'm guessing you'll want to do the same with my parents."

She nodded. The people closest to them would not be left out of this ruse. Ellie wouldn't be that unfair or unkind.

"Tomorrow we go get the license," Shane stated.

"Okay," she said. She was exhausted from this battle and desperate for it to end.

"But for now," Shane said and pulled her closer, "let's celebrate naked-bodies style."

20

THURSDAY

After her standard morning—diner, deliveries, and the Williamses' ranch—Ellie and Shane drove to Bison's Prairie to get a marriage license. They chose to go outside their town in hopes of delaying any retaliation from whoever was at the helm of all Ellie's troubles. Ellie and Shane wanted to be married, then let the world know.

Telling Grams and Shane's family the plan had been both humiliating and humbling. Even though she felt as if she was getting the better end of the deal, taking advantage of Shane's kindness, his parents hadn't appeared to feel that at all. They were more upset by the news that he would be returning to active duty within the next week. Dottie had cast Ellie a look that spoke of her desperation to keep Shane home, as if Ellie actually had any pull to make that happen. Her faith in Ellie was humbling. Misplaced for sure. Ellie had no more influence over Shane's decisions than the ocean's tide had over the moon.

Grams had nodded once and told Ellie her heart and gut should guide her. Ellie had a hard time listening to her heart and gut since fear had such a strong and angry voice that boomed over everything else.

Shane and Ellie's friends would be headed over in the evening. A simple ceremony, officiated by Sabrina, would be held outside in the backyard. Until then, Ellie needed to get away, to put distance between herself and the chaos of her life. She saddled Winnie, her paint, and rode up into the foothills where her grandfather had found a large sapphire all those years back. She wasn't going to mine for stones. Only sit and try to be close to her ancestors. Maybe she'd get some advice on the wind. Most people turned to their parents for help and guidance. Ellie hadn't bothered. She'd have better luck with ghosts.

At her destination, Ellie sat with her back against the large boulder that had tumbled down the mountain years ago. She let Winnie graze. Not that there was much grass since the terrain in this area was rockier. These hills held secrets. The mountains stood like sentries and guarded those secrets. So much was buried within: diamonds, gold, jade, sapphires, and even dinosaur fossils. One day, she would be buried among it all, her story with her. And try as she might to reconcile all the options before her, she couldn't see any possible alternative to life other than staying on the farm and making it work. Ellie was too stubborn for less. Would she look back at this decision to marry Shane with regret or relief?

She heard the whinny of a horse and glanced at Winnie. Her ears were pinned back, and she stood motionless, her attention on the top of the hill. Ellie stood and looked over the boulder into a copse of trees. Norris Landry rode into the break.

He waved a hand in greeting. "What brings you out this way?" he called as his horse picked his way through the rough ground.

"Just came here to think. I like how quiet it is out here. How about you, Uncle Norris?" His saddlebags were bulging, a pick ax hung from a leather loop of the side bag.

"I was doing a check on our lands and fence line, saw you

across the way. Can't be too cautious, especially after all the stuff you've been going through." He pulled back the reigns, and once his horse settled, he slid off. "How you feeling? That was some accident."

Ellie gave a haphazard shrug. Norris still talked to her dad so she was careful about what she said. "It could have been worse. I'm feeling pretty good. More shook up than anything."

Norris came to stand beside her and leaned against the boulder. He carried a water bottle with him. It was moments like this that Ellie missed her dad. Standing on their family's property, looking out at the scenic view after a day of hard work and horseback riding, had been Ellie's dream. Bitterly, she thought it was funny she was expected to live her father's dream and ignore her own. Somewhat, Norris Landry filled the void her father had created.

"It's a sight to behold, isn't it?" Uncle Norris said and wiped his forehead with the back of his shirtsleeve.

"I never get tired of looking at it." She faced him. "Any damage to your property?"

He shook his head. "I hate you're going through this, Ellie. I have to admit it worries me, and I'm not above wanting you to leave. Go be with your folks and be safe. I think of you like a niece, and I'm concerned. My dad is, too."

Ellie nodded. "Only I don't want to be a missionary, Uncle Norris. I want this." She swept her hand wide to indicate her family's farm.

He shook his head sadly. "I think that's the hardest part of growing up, reconciling dreams with reality."

She didn't like anyone telling her she couldn't have what she wanted out of life. "Makes me feel like a quitter," Ellie mumbled.

"No one would think of you as a quitter. What are you expected to do? Many a rancher and farmer have folded up and moved on. Mrs. Zykowski loves living in town. More time to do what she wants. She's much happier now that she's not tied to the ranch she had."

Ellie wanted to point out the Mrs. Z was Grams age. When a fire had taken her ranch away, Mrs. Z had made lemonade out of some really crappy lemons. That last point was all Ellie and Mrs. Z had in common.

"I'm not ready to give in," Ellie told him.

Uncle Norris sighed with dejection, his mouth a thin press of his lips. "I figured you'd say that. You are, after all, your father's daughter. I hope you have a plan."

"Shane has a few ideas." Ellie wasn't ready to tip her hand to anyone.

Uncle Norris snorted. "Shane Hannigan is like his dad. A taker. How do you think Shawn Hannigan got so successful with his ranch?" He didn't wait for her to answer. "He saw opportunity—like, say, when a rancher was down on his luck—and swooped in."

"Even if that is true about his father 'swooping in,' what's that got to do with Shane? He's not working with his father." Ellie knew the Hannigan's plan was for Shane to do is thing and then take over the ranch when he retired from active duty. It was no secret.

"Because he's been away, but now what? What's he going to do if he can't go back to the service and do what he was trained to do?" Uncle Norris raised a bushy dark brow. He looked worried, and Ellie's heart was softened by his concern.

Shane had warned her to keep mum about his plans. She wasn't to tell anyone outside their circle. She saw no harm in telling the avuncular man she'd know most her life, but kept her lips sealed anyway. "I guess we'll know in due time," she said.

Uncle Norris scratched his chin. "Something to think about. Shane may be trying to get his hands on your farm." He raised both brushy brows so they met in the middle like a giant fuzzy strip.

Ellie barked out a laugh. "Why would Shane want the farm? He's going to take over one of the biggest ranches in the state."

"Not anytime soon. His dad's not ready to retire, and what's Shane supposed to do in the meantime? Work as a reporter for his sister?" Uncle Norris laughed.

Ellie tried to picture it and laughed with him. She shook her head. "No, I can't see that either. But what would he do with our farm?"

Uncle Norris played with the cap to his water. "Turn it into his own ranch. Maybe it would be a hobby for him. Something to do until he gets the real deal. You have to admit you have good land. Your crop space could be turned into decent pastures. You all weren't hit by the fire as hard as we were or some of the others." He nudged her with his elbow and chuckled. "And you got this here land rich with gems and gold."

Ellie swept her hand in front of them, gesturing to the rugged earth. "Oh, totally. It's spitting out high dollar sapphires left and right. Can't you see us rolling in them?" It took a lot for her not to roll her eyes. "I'm not one to chase get-rich-quick ideas, and though this land produced something once, doesn't mean it will again."

Uncle Norris looked like he wanted to say something, but he pressed his lips together then frowned. "Just watch your back. Sometimes things aren't what they seem."

Ellie stood next to him and dropped her head to his shoulder. "I'll be careful. I promise. Thanks for looking out for us."

"You and Grams are like family to me. Of course, I'll look after you." Uncle Norris kissed the top of her head. "You two decide to go live a more relaxed life, you better give me first dibs on the land."

Ellie straightened, surprised by the request. The Landrys had never mentioned wanting to expand or showed any interest in the Greenes' land. "I suppose I should get going." She whistled for Winnie.

Uncle Norris said, "I saw some trucks headed down to the farm. You having a party?"

Ellie shook her head. She didn't want to outright lie. "We're having friends over."

The way Uncle Norris studied her was unnerving. As if he knew she wasn't being completely truthful. Ellie turned her attention on Winnie.

Without looking at him, she said, "We should have dinner soon," extending an olive branch of sorts.

"I'd love that," he said and waved as Ellie pointed Winnie toward home.

She was halfway home when an odd thought popped into her mind. If Uncle Norris had been checking his property, how had he seen people coming to the farm? The Landry ranch was to the northwest of the Greenes' farm. The Greenes' driveway was to the southeast of their house and barn. Aside from the house and barn blocking the view, there were also the rolling foothills and the forest.

Her concern for Uncle Norris aside, a large more disturbing thought bloomed. Was Uncle Norris right about Shane? What if Shane was given incorrect information, and he wouldn't be returning to active duty? What would he do then? Ellie wasn't sure, but one thing was for certain, should Shane's plans change, their impending nuptials would give him all rights to the farm. He would most certainly get something from this wedding after all.

THURSDAY

When Ellie rode into the meadow leading to the farm, she saw two things—everyone had arrived but no one was around. She led Winnie to the pasture and removed her saddle to let her graze. She refreshed the trough and, with saddle thrown over her arm, headed to the barn to retrieve carrots. Ellie liked to reward Winnie with a handful while she brushed her down. When Shane came from around the corner near the goat pen, Ellie jumped.

"Hi," Shane said.

"Hi." Uncle Norris's warnings dashed through her mind.

"Do you have a second?" Shane asked. He was dressed like she'd first seen him. His jeans were dark wash, and he wore a tucked in green flannel shirt over a navy T. His boots were the black ones he favored.

Ellie glanced at Winnie and then to the saddle on her arm. "Can we walk and talk?"

"Sure, but I need a quick gut check from you." Shane tried to catch her eye, but she managed to avoid it.

Ellie didn't like the sound of that. Shane's smile was calm, almost placid, but his eyes crinkled slightly which told of worry. Shane attempted to help when Ellie lifted the saddle, but she shifted around him and brought it down to rest on the fence that separated the yard from the pasture Ellie and Shane were standing in.

Ellie crossed her arms, dug deep for inner strength, and faced him. "Gut check about what?" Because right now, Ellie's gut was a churning mess. Uncle Norris's words and her doubts and fears were all mixed together making a hotbed of stress.

"When we decided to do this thing, we decided to keep it simple."

"What thing is that?" She decided to poke the bear, wondering if the term he'd use would be "business deal."

Shane shook his head and surprised her by going in a different direction. "I'm sorry. I don't mean to call it less than it is. Only, I'm not sure how you want to refer to us getting married. I kinda thought we needed to keep it more business-like. Or simple."

"We need to keep it that way or you do?" Could her "minor farm incidents" been just pranks, but the rest was Shane stepping in to capitalize on an opportunity as Uncle Norris suggested? Or was she mad because he wanted to leave and this was her way of letting him go? She certainly felt foolish for hoping he'd stay, and being angry was far easier to deal with than being weepy and blue. Ellie wanted to groan with frustration and regret and maybe kick something. Everything was such a mess.

"Hey, what's going on here? Why are you so upset?" Shane reached for her, but she sidestepped and held her palm out to stop him from coming closer.

"I'm upset because my life is a chaos. Because people want things from me, and they aren't being truthful about what those things are!" She stepped away.

Shane straightened and jerked a thumb toward his chest. "Are you talking about me? I came over here to tell you my sister and Hannah are in your backyard decorating the shit out of it, trying to make it all fancy, and I was thinking that might make you real uncomfortable."

"I don't want that," Ellie said. "We aren't playing house."

"I agree." He crossed his arms over his chest, his biceps bulging. Lord, even when she was afraid he might be conning her she lusted for him. She was so pathetic.

"This is me with few options, and I thought this was you helping out the best way you could." Ellie kicked at the dirt. "Heck, I'm not sure I even want to do this, Shane."

Shane's eyes narrowed. "What do you mean you thought this was me helping the best I could? That's exactly what I'm doing. I'm trying to protect you. Can I ask what changed?"

Ellie glanced over her shoulder to where she'd just ridden. She shook her head to try to clear the ugly words and doubts from her mind. "Nothing. Just some thinking and speculating."

Shane glanced toward the foothills. "Did you run into someone there?"

Ellie bit her lip. Inside, she had so many secrets and thoughts that she didn't know whom she could trust anymore. She was questioning everyone and everything. Earlier today, she'd been sure of her decision and that, as crazy as it seemed, marrying Shane was the best option. Borrowing his name as protection while still giving her the chance to solve her problems wasn't a bad idea. The added bonus would be telling her dad to go shove Brad off on someone else, she was taken. She would happily omit that her married state was temporary.

Shane sighed and relaxed his stance. "Look, Ellie. I know we don't have years together under our belts, but you know me. So I hope you will give my next words deep consideration. Relationships, not only romantic ones, but friendships and those with family, parents etcetera fail for one of two reasons." He held up two fingers. "Compromise and communication. I like to think if nothing else, we've become good friends."

He didn't wait for her to acknowledge. He continued, "Often

people compromise without adequate communication. This builds resentment. Compromise shouldn't be sacrifice. Communication removes that. Talk to me. Whatever it is you're feeling right now is okay, but share it with me so I can help."

Ellie shook her head. "I don't even know what I'm feeling." Fear, confusion, heartbreak, or love? Ellie's insides pitched. Her heart skipped a beat as she realized that love was a high possibility. She pressed her hands to her cheeks, trying to hold back the heat of embarrassment. Everything she said she would never do, she'd done. She'd fallen for a man who had no interest in staying. She'd fallen for a man who loved the adventure of the unknown more than the adventure of farming and ranching.

Ellie blinked several times, forcing back the tears. "You need to tell the others to stop decorating. There's not going to be a wedding." She brushed her thumbs under her eyes to wipe away the moisture and moved to skirt around him.

"Dammit Ellie, you cannot just run from me. What the hell is going on?" His voice raised in frustration.

"I can't do this, Shane," she cried.

"Talk to me." He snaked out an arm and caught her before she could get past him.

"Let me go. I've changed my mind. You need to go back to the Marines free and clear." She refused to look at him. Afraid he would see what she was really feeling, and more afraid that behind the love she was broadcasting, he'd see doubt.

"Always running away. One day you're gonna find the man you want to hold on to and he might be the one to run from you. I guess Brad and I have something in common now." His tone was bitter.

Ellie jerked like she'd been slapped. She narrowed her eyes, words at the ready, a need to fight back rising within her. Then something by the barn caught her eye.

Ellie straightened, all her attention on the side of the barn where she'd seen the movement. She squinted, not believing her eyes.

Shane noticing her attention had shifted and turned to look in the direction she was staring. "Are those what I think they are?"

Mute by shock, Ellie nodded. She was counting heads. One or two rats were common. Four at once meant there were more. More meant there was trouble.

"Rats," Shane whispered.

They scurried alongside the barn and had found a hide-y-hole or tunnel that was under the barn.

Ellie jerked her arm free. "Go get the rifle from the house. Tell Grams." She took off at a run, vaulting over the fence. Inside the barn she surveyed the space, concentrating. She had to look past the stalls, storage room, and tack lined walls to get a bead on where the rats were coming in. Realization dawned. They were in the feed room. Rats liked grain and seed. Both of those and hay were stored in the feed room. Ellie, having no interest in battling rats, had continued with her grandparents' philosophy and kept everything stored in metal rat-proof boxes. Even horse and goat blankets were stored that way. She cleaned the barn every other day. There were traps placed along walls in the barn as a precaution, and for three years now they'd had...maybe two...incidents with rats. Maybe a few more with mice.

Ellie flung open the door to the feed room and screamed.

Rats were everywhere. This wasn't just a few who'd come from the fields. This was an infestation. Large brown rats were happily stuffing their faces with seed and grain. The boxes she'd used to store the feed and grain were tipped over, lid flung across the room. No rat had done this.

Ellie backed up. In the tack room, she kept a .22 pellet rifle. It was older than dirt and hadn't been used in a while, but Ellie didn't care. If it didn't fire anymore, then she'd use the thing as a bat and take some swings at the foul rodents. She dashed to the room and pulled the rifle off the shelf from behind some tack. In the drawer, she found pellets and quickly loaded the rifle. Ellie knew this wasn't the solution, but she needed to do something, anything. Picking a few off might scare the others and give them time to clean up the mess. Then she could try and bait and trap the rest.

Forcing herself to calm down. Ellie sat crossed legged on the floor outside the feed room and raised the rifle to take aim. She'd taken four down when Shane came running in.

"Ellie," he shouted and pulled her up by her arm, "the farm stand is on fire."

Ellie, who'd kept the rifle aimed at the rats, let her arm and the gun drop. "What?" she asked, not processing what he'd said.

"Cori noticed smoke coming from near the road. Fort went to check it out. He said the stand is on fire. He's called the fire station. They're on their way." He pulled her toward him, leading her out of the building. Shane pushed her toward his truck where Cricket was at the wheel. After shoving her into the cab, he climbed in behind her and hadn't closed the door before Cricket peeled out, speeding to the top of the mile-long drive.

Sure enough, the farm stand was engulfed in flames. The only thing anyone could do was watch it burn while they waited for the fire truck. The hose they used to rinse the fruits and vegetables was unreachable, surrounded by flames.

Ellie saw Grams standing beside Hannah, her face wet with tears.

Ellie went to her. "I'm sorry, Grams. I'm sorry I brought this on us."

Grams folded her in a hug. "Hush, child. You didn't do this. Some maniac did. I can't imagine what this person wants. Clearly, it's not the farm if they're burning down parts of it," Grams said while rubbing Ellie's back.

The fire engine arrived and managed to hook up the water. Slowly, they combated the fire.

Shane, who stood next to Grams and Ellie, waved over Fort.

"The other day I went to Mr. Phillips's place. He was having a rat issue. Building traps for them. Any chance he could have done this?"

Ellie shrugged. She wouldn't put anything past anyone anymore.

Grams shook her head. "Lester Phillips is a character, but there's no mean streak in his body. After what he'd seen in the war, I can't imagine him doing this."

Minutes later, the fire was contained and slowly dwindling. Only a third of the stand remained.

"We'll rebuild it," Shane said. "That part is easy."

"You'll have to wait until an investigation is over," Fort said. "Clearly this is a case of arson." He pointed to a partially melted red gasoline can. "In the meantime, let's go have a conversation with Lester Phillips."

Ellie with her arms around her grandmother pointed to a truck approaching. "Here he comes now."

Lester's newer Ford came to a screeching halt across the road, sending gravel spraying. He jumped from the truck and hustled over to them at an impressive tick for a man his age.

"Jumping Aunt Hannah, I heard on my scanner there was a fire here. I came as soon as I could." He rushed to Grams. "You okay, Minnie?" He scanned her quickly. "You look okay. You breathe any of the smoke in? Need me to get you an ambulance? You were here, right? Did you see what happened?" He put his hands on his hips and sucked in a breath. "Jeez, gave this old man's ticker some arrhythmia." He thumbed his chest.

Ellie watched Mr. Phillips, the tight press of his mouth, the worried furrow of his brows. Her mind put the pieces together until she finally saw the puzzle picture fully. Mr. Phillips had a crush on Grams.

"Who would do something like this, Lester?" Grams said and took his hand. "I can't begin to fathom."

He shook his head.

Shane cleared his throat. "Mr. Phillips, remember all them rats you had in your barn? Did you manage to trap them?"

Mr. Phillips said a curse word then spat on the ground. "I trapped about a dozen. You think that makes a difference? Nope, more just take their place. I think someone's sabotaging me."

Shane cast a skeptical look toward Mr. Phillips and caught Fort's eye. Ellie watched it all unfold.

Listen to your gut.

These words had been her maxim since Shane had shown up. And her gut told her Mr. Phillips might be a radical conspiracy theorist, but he wasn't their nemesis. He wasn't the source of their problems.

She asked, "Why do you think someone's sabotaging you?"

"Came home yesterday to find someone had dumped out my grain bin. Saw trail of it leading out from the barn. Or to the barn —suppose that depends on how you see things."

Fort crossed his arms over his chest. "What do you think they want?"

"My land. I think it's those hippy students digging for fool's gold or whatever they think is on my land." Mr. Phillips chuckled and winked at Shane. "Member I told you about my piece of gold. Well, those idiots haven't found a thing. They were on my land all day yesterday, and they said no one stopped by or anything. Except, I can't see those rats tipping over a bin of grain and managing my sliding bolt latch. They'd need opposable thumbs to lift and slide." Mr. Phillips showed us his thumbs.

"Why didn't you call the police?" Fort asked.

Phillips chuckled. "I took care of it. I kicked them off the land." He elbowed Shane. "So much for their projects. The real good land is here, Minnie's land."

"Why do you say that?" Fort asked.

"Because not only does she have those gems, but I bet she has natural gas like me." Phillips poked a thumb in his puffed out chest.

173

Shane leaned in. "What do you mean natural gas like you?"

Phillips chuckled. "Bob Williams and I email all the time. He gets homesick. He was talking about the natural gas found on his land and said I should have mine looked into. Well, when those students came out to do whatever the hell it was they did besides leave a mess, I had some guy come and test. Sure enough, I got me some natural gas, too. Thinking about selling some of my land rights and banking the money." He eyed Grams. "Thinking I might have something nice to offer to a special woman."

Ellie interrupted, "Wait, could this whole sabotage business be over natural gas?" She tried to connect the dots.

"Sure, why not? Natural gas equates to money. Those snotty college kids looking for gold were too dumb to realize the boulder rolled down hill, and all the while they were sitting on natural gas. Jokes on them, and I had a good laugh." He chuckled again.

Fort crossed his arms. "Until someone gave you rats. Now the jokes on you."

Phillips's smile fell. "Well, there is that."

Ellie shook her head. "No, the joke has been on us the entire time. I think I figured out what's going on."

22

SATURDAY

After much debate, Ellie, Grams, Shane, and Fort had finally agreed to a plan of action to end the sabotage once and for all. And coming to an agreement had only taken two days. Fort called it a sting operation. Shane called it closure. Ellie didn't care what anyone called it; she wanted the night over with so she could get on with her life. Mess that it was. She didn't have any answers or solutions to the financial problems she and Grams still faced, and with the farm store gone... *One problem at a time.*

Shane patted her side again, feeling the small handgun he'd strapped to her via a shoulder holster.

"It hasn't gone anywhere," she told him without meeting his eyes.

"I'm simply double-checking," he said quietly.

Things had been strained between them since the fire. Trying to get over the hurdle of awful words they'd flung at each other out in the pasture had been complicated by the official word from Shane's med board. He was allowed to return to active duty. He was expected to report to camp Pendleton by the middle of next week. His new job, instructor at sniper school, was vastly different than being in the field. Ellie couldn't tell what he thought about his new path with the Marines. He wasn't saying much. In fact, once the scheme was decided, Shane had made himself scarce.

After the fire, Ellie had shared her suspicions with Fort and Shane and Grams. They'd been hard to swallow, and part of her hoped that tonight she would be proven wrong.

Shane tugged her jacket together. "Set up camp right away. Do some hammering to scare off any bears, keep your spray nearby."

Ellie nodded. "We've been through this. I'll do everything I can to make it look like I'm onto something."

"Mr. Phillips has seeded the soil at the diner last night. It's game time." Shane tapped her earbud, and she turned it on.

"Test, test," Shane's voice came through the tiny wireless inductive receiver in her ear.

Ellie kinda felt like Grams without the high-screeching pitch. "I feel bad about putting Mr. Phillips's name on my suspect list." Short as the list was, he'd been on top.

"Don't," Fort said. He was already out in the field, setting up his watch point. He was connected to them through an earpiece. "Only feel bad when you publicly accuse someone without proof and destroy their lives."

Ellie nodded. She knew Fort couldn't see her but Shane could.

"Okay," Shane said, "I'm sending her out. I'll leave ten minutes after her and should be in place thirty minutes after that."

"Its go time," Fort said.

Ellie strode out of the house without a farewell or a backward glance. Tears threatened to fall. Once this thing, this sting operation was over, Shane would be gone. They would smoke out the person trying to destroy her, and his job would be done. He could go back to the life he wanted, and she could stay in hers.

So why did the thought of it make her so sad? Because she

loved the stupid man? Likely. Because she was too stubborn to change or bend? Even more likely.

Ellie rode Winnie into the foothills, going back to the place where her Gramps had found his sapphire. She let Winnie graze while she set up camp, just like she was directed. Though she was heated from the exertion, she kept her jacket on, her handgun concealed.

Randomly selecting a spot to pretend dig, Ellie roped off a small square, three by three, and began breaking up the land like she'd seen in the geology YouTube videos she'd watched. She wanted to take a hammer to the area, even a blowtorch. But she needed to play this game out. She needed her enemy to believe she was desperately seeking gems of any sort. She needed them to think she might have found something. She hoped it would be just one more reason for them to want the Greenes' land and would be enough to smoke the person out.

Ellie worked diligently, her mind on a thousand things, her attention not on her task. When Shane spoke, she jumped and had to catch herself from looking in the direction where he lay in wait.

"You're being watched," he'd said.

Shane was in the hills concealed by an old hunting blind covering her back with his sniper rifle, Fort was hidden in the trees of rocky terrain up a hill and across a meadow. Ellie had thought Shane was taking the plan too far, but then she'd been reminded of the stranger in the truck.

Game on.

Ellie wasn't much of an actress, but she poured all her frustration into her role to pretend to find something of value. She inspected the land, looking a second time with a magnifying glass. She then rushed to Winnie and dug out a book from her saddlebag, dropping it to show nervousness and excitement. The first she didn't have to fake, her nerves were frayed, tension a tightly coiled ball sitting between her shoulders. Ellie compared the picture in the book to the dirt and the nubby rock that was protruding. The rock was nothing more than a ball of clay, but from a distance, no one would know that. Even with binoculars.

Ellie glanced around like she'd seen people in the movies do when they were on to something big and wanted to hide it. She covered the clay with dirt she'd removed earlier. She tied a ribbon to the sagebrush closest to the tiny mound then strung a string from the ribbon to the heap as a way to measure the location. Ellie cut the string then tucked it in a baggie and back into her saddlebag.

The person watching her would have to be a fool to believe she managed to find something BIG in the short time she'd been up here, but Fort had said desperation made people believe the weirdest things, and she had to believe him. He saw all kinds of crazy in his job as sheriff. Ellie went about making a second dig site, the second part of the plan, hoping it would plant the idea that Grams's hills were loaded.

After making three dig sites, the plan was to have Ellie stay the night. This is the part Shane didn't like and, truthfully, Ellie didn't either. But Fort had said that by Ellie staying, it showed she was protecting what she'd found, and whatever it was had a value. In the morning, she would pretend to struggle to raise anyone on the radio or phone and would act uncertain about being forced to go back home to get assistance, leaving her findings unprotected. The goal was to raise her enemy's eagerness to get to Ellie's secret findings, opening up the opportunity for her antagonist to come out from hiding and be caught. What they didn't know was if her enemy would send a hired hand or be the person themselves. So the waiting began.

Ellie acted out her measuring skit three more times, the last for good measure. Evening was pushing the day into the hills, announcing its intention, making way for the dark of night. There were only a few more hours of light left. Ellie tried not to count the hours until this would be over. Instead, she built a fire and settled in to eat dinner and call it a night. She might actually sleep knowing Bryce, Fort, and Shane were out there. They'd called in backup help from Shane's father and Deke Sutton, who used to be a deputy.

She'd just strung up her bear bag and was walking back to camp when she heard a twig snap. Ellie hesitated then remembered something Shane had warned about tipping her hand. She needed to pretend she wasn't expecting anything but wildlife.

"Hey bear," she called. "Go away bear." It was something she would have done any other time. Ellie started singing an old bible favorite of Grams.

"Go tell it on the mountain," she crooned while slowly making her way to camp.

"I can't see anything," Shane told her through the earbud. "It might be an animal. Might not. Your watcher is gone."

"Could you see who it was?" she asked quietly.

"Not from my angle," Shane said.

"Mine either." It was Deke in place of Fort.

"This is going to be the longest night," she told them.

Shane grunted his agreement.

Ellie watched the sun dip low behind the foothills, the orange sky being compressed by the navy blue of night. The stars the only light besides the tangerine flames of her fire.

She didn't need a book or any other sort of distraction. Watching night stretch out its arms and wrap them around the mountains was breathtaking. How anyone would want to look at anything else was inconceivable.

"I've missed this," Shane said in her ear. He'd been quiet for a while, and Ellie wondered if he'd taken a break. She'd doubted it. She hadn't taken one and knew he wouldn't do less than her.

Ellie stretched, lifting her hands over her head, about to tell her earbud pals she was calling it a night when a rustle came from the woods to her right. She went still, straining to hear something more.

She lowered her arms slowly, bringing one hand to move inside her coat for the gun and the other to find the snap that would release her bear spray.

The bushes rustled again, no doubt whatever was making them move wasn't the wind.

Ellie wasn't sure how to alert the guys that she wasn't alone. Her gut said whatever it was flanking her right side wasn't wildlife. There was something more familiar about the sound. Like someone pushing the bushes aside instead of plowing through them.

Ellie eased from the chair and said, "Hey bear. Hey bear." She turned to face the direction of the sound.

"Hang on, switching to thermal imaging," Shane said. A beat went by, and then he swore. "Its a person."

"Um…." Ellie stood still. "Hey bear," she said weakly. She took her finger off the spray then eased the handgun from the holster. The hairs on the back of her neck stood in warning and were vibrating from the tension running through her body.

"He's coming toward you," Shane said.

"Be cool," Deke added. "We're right here. I've already called back Fort." But right here was seventy-five yards away for the both of them.

"I know what you're thinking, cute-face," Shane said. "But I can solve this problem with the flick of finger. You're safe. If I can't get a clear shot, I'll let you know."

Oddly, Ellie didn't find comfort in knowing someone could be shot. All this nonsense was coming to what she hoped wouldn't be an ugly outcome.

More noise from the woods, and this time a twig broke. Ellie crossed her arms, tucking the tiny gun under her forearm, obscuring it from view. The dark night helped.

"Who's there?" she called.

"Ellie?" This time the voice wasn't in her ear. It came from the direction of the noise. "Ellie, is that you?" The figure stepped out from the tree coverage.

Norris Landry. She'd hoped it wouldn't be. Not that any other alternative was better.

Ellie feigned relief and backed up to her chair. She wanted to sit and not block Shane.

Norris Landry had been the one deflating her tires, breaking her irrigator, and allowed—no, setup her goats to be attacked.

She wanted to charge at him, catch him with her head to his middle, and knock him over. She wanted to pound against him and get the answers she sorely deserved. Now she understood why men punched people in the face.

"Is that you, Norris?" She couldn't bring herself to call him uncle. Uncles didn't bring harm and hate to people they loved.

"What are you doing out here?" Norris stepped a few feet closer, moving into a sliver of cast-off light from the fire. He was dressed in dark clothes. Not something people did when in the woods at night. Unless they were hoping not to be seen. A dark ski cap sat on the top of his head.

"I needed to get away from the farm. After the fire and all, well...I needed to clear my head." It wasn't a complete lie.

"And you came here?" He stood with his hands in the oversize pockets of his jacket, and the bulge on the right side was bigger than a lone fist. Gun maybe?

Ellie gave a bitter laugh. "Well, we could use some luck. Ya know, I thought about what you said about the gems out here and thought maybe Gramps might smile down on me and lead me to some gold or something. I hear Lester Phillips found some on his property."

Norris snorted with derision, his stance ramrod straight, as if he might snap from excessive tension. "He's a fool. That gold came from a boulder that tumbled onto his land."

"I imagine tracing it would be hard," Ellie said.

Landry shook his head. "Not for a geologist."

"Like you," Ellie finished.

"Exactly." Landry shifted his weight, his posture changed. He looked more like the slump-shouldered surrogate father he'd played. "Listen, Ellie. I know the timing is bad on this, but I'm guessing after the fire, you and Minnie could use some money. Pops and I would like to help you out." He waved a hand to stop her from saying anything. "But before you refuse, let me say it's not a handout. We'd like to buy this upper land from you. It's really only good for pasture land, and you're not grazing this far out, right?"

The line of bullshit was so smooth she almost didn't recognize it. But there's no way to cover the odor of poop, and this pile stunk to high heaven.

Ellie went for the punch to the solar plexus. "Well, I dunno. I just found some gems up here. Maybe this land is more valuable than I think."

Norris's expression was blank. Not what Ellie had been hoping for. Was it not gems he wanted?

He shook his head and sighed with disgust. "Pops and I will let you come dig your naive little heart out if you want. While we own it. If these little shiny pocket rocks mean so much to you. If you think they'll change your life, go for it." He swept his hand across the land. "Dig away."

Ellie was puzzled. Her assumption had been that Norris Landry wanted the Greenes' land for the mining of gems, but he didn't care about the gems. Her brain provided the answer right as Shane said it in her ear.

"Natural gas."

Ellie sat forward, her elbows on her knees, and hands tucked under her pits. "Gosh, I wish you had said something sooner. I'm already in negotiations regarding the mineral rights. The deal is pretty good. I wish I had thought of it sooner."

"No!" Landry roared and charged away from the trees toward her before coming to a stop as sudden as his outburst. He stood on the far side of the fire, anger etching the lines of his face, narrowing his eyes as he stared at her.

Ellie sat back. "Um...."

He waved his hands in the air as if trying to wipe away any residue of his explosion. "I mean, don't do that. Please. It's not good for the environment. It's not good for Wolf Creek. I could give you a thousand arguments as to why it's a bad idea." He shuffled closer, leaving only the small fire separating them.

Ellie was tired of the runaround. "A thousand arguments, but none would be the truth." Her gun was warm against her skin. She thought she'd be more scared, but a rod of bravado rushed through her. She was tired. She was beyond frustrated. She was ready for this to be over and to resume her normal life. Whatever that might look like. She'd forgotten how she'd existed before all this had started.

"What does that mean?" His head was slightly ducked and he looked up at her from under his brows. With the flicker of the fire casting shadows, he appeared menacing.

"Don't bait him," Fort cautioned. "Maybe try getting him to confess by using honey instead of vinegar?"

Ellie swallowed. She ignored the advice. "It means you want this land, and not for grazing either. You burned down our farm stand, didn't you?" Ellie stood, her blood beginning a rapid boil. "You were the one who broke the lock that allowed that coyote in. Aren't you?" She dropped her arms, the gun rest against her leg.

"Now, Ellie..."

"Don't you 'now Ellie' me. You sat at our table, and while we fed you and shared our concerns and fears, you were planning on using those weaknesses against us. We trusted you,"

She was yelling so she steadied herself and lowered her voice. "Here's what's going to happen," she bluffed. "I'm going to lease out my mineral rights." Ellie pointed her index finger at him. "You will get nothing from this land. Nothing from us. I will make sure of that."

From his pocket, Landry pulled out his hand, a small handgun like hers clutched in his meaty fist. "I'm holding all the cards here," he said in a low, angry voice.

"You going to shoot me, *Uncle* Norris? How will you explain that? What will you do after that? Go down and shoot Grams, too? You might be able to make mine look like a wildlife attack but what about Grams?" Ellie's knees quivered, but she held steady.

"Cute-face," came the voice in her ear, "I need you to get out of the way. Back up one step and to the right. Take the chair with you. Don't turn your back to him. Then sit down."

"You have no idea what you are talking about, Ellie. No idea. Just sign over the land and this can be all over." Landry's hand shook as he yelled and pointed the gun at her.

Ellie was afraid he might accidentally discharge the weapon. She made quick work of Shane's request and nearly collapsed in the chair.

She tried to look unfazed. "I will never sell this land to you. Never," she spit out.

Landry pulled back the hammer of his gun, the click echoing across the space.

This was the moment, the one where her life was supposed to flash before her eyes, but Ellie was too shocked for her brain to process anything. One second she was wondering how she'd gotten to this point, and the next a shot rang out across the valley.

Ellie flinched, squeezed her eyes closed, and braced herself for what she expected to be agonizing pain.

Nothing.

She opened her eyes. Norris Landry was no longer standing before her. He was on the ground moaning.

Ellie jumped up and ran to him. His hand was over his right shoulder, blood seeping into the ground. His gun had fallen to the side so she kicked it away.

"You shot me," he said angrily.

"Not me. Shane." She pointed over her shoulder in the direction of Shane's blind. "From way over there. We've been waiting for you." She pulled off her jacket and removed her flannel shirt. After balling it up, she placed it on Landry's shoulder, using the opportunity to press down into the wound, knowing it would cause him more pain.

Landry moaned.

"You did all those things to us just to get our land. All because you want the rights. Why?" She shook her head in disbelief.

"I was desperate. Our ranch is suffering. We're nearly bankrupt. Pops left the management to me, and I've driven it into the ground." He grimaced, and his eyes rolled back in his head.

"Oh, no you don't," she told him. "You don't get to pass out." She pressed harder, and he arched from the pain. But he was more alert.

"What made you decide to harass us instead of simply asking us to sell or split the cost with you?"

Landry laughed, coughed, then winced. "Oh, that wasn't my idea. It wasn't until all that started that I saw an opportunity to kill two birds with one stone."

"Who's idea was it? Who wants us out of business more than you?"

Landry coughed again, then met her gaze. "Your father."

23

2 MONTHS LATER

Having learned her father was the mastermind behind the harassment had shattered Ellie's world. His saving grace, or more Ellie's forgiving heart, had come in admitting he'd been trying to get Grams to sell so Ellie would come back and be with her parents. Her father confessed he canceled the feed store order, and he'd sworn all he'd asked Norris to do were the little things like letting out the air in her tires and disabling the irrigation system. Norris Landry had taken it a step further. Each time. Even hiring the man in the truck. Just like Fort said, desperation did that to a person.

Deke Sutton had done some digging using his government connections and discovered the elder Landry had sold his OG&M rights in a hundred-year contract. Either the company would need to go out of business or more years needed to pass before Norris Landry could make money off his land's oil, gas, or minerals. The sabotage had never been about gemstones or gold. Only the potential for money. The possibility of natural gas and a fat wallet. Yes, she had pressed charges. Silver lining to all this was now her dad was off her back. He'd finally heard her when she said she didn't want to be like them and now was supporting her, in the best way he could.

Ellie sat in the pasture while the goats ran around her. Benny was back and stronger than ever, his cart bumping behind him as he chased Bad Bad Leroy Brown. Leroy liked a good game of tag, and Benny was it.

Run Around Sue head-butted Ellie. Ellie laughed and scratched her between the ears. The farm had come a long way in the three months since that night in the foothills. In full agreement, Ellie and Grams had made a deal with a company to lease some of their land. If natural gas were to be found, should the OG&M company even decide to explore, then the Greenes would get royalties in addition to the rental money. This was the option they felt suited them best. Outright selling the land wasn't even a consideration.

Summer was in full swing. Many of the crops were coming in. The good people, Shane included, had joined rebuilding the farm stand. That was the last time she'd seen him. The next morning while working at the diner, Cricket had informed her that Shane was back on the road, California his destination. His absence was a gut punch to the solar plexus. She'd been mad there was no goodbye, but the truth was she couldn't have handled one. She was glad he'd slipped away. Mostly.

Ellie tried not to dwell on it. She'd started and discarded several emails. Letting go was the best choice. Staying in touch was holding on, and holding on did nothing but make her heart ache more.

The crunch of tires on their gravel drive forced Ellie's attention off her thoughts of Shane an onto the sheriff's brown and white pickup headed toward her. She extracted herself from her goats and walked toward the house. Grams was on the porch, gently rocking in her chair while she knitted and whistled. She glanced from the truck to Ellie.

Ellie shrugged her answer. She wasn't expecting a visit from law enforcement. She waited at the bottom of the stairs for Fort.

Grams sighed heavily, stopped knitting, then preceded to put in her hearing aids.

Fort parked the truck and approached. When he was close enough, Grams held out her hand to stop him from speaking. "Hang on, one more second, and I'll have these things up and running." She pointed to her ear.

Fort smiled and nodded. "How you doing, Ellie?" Though he cut a fine figure in his uniform, broad-shouldered and trim waist, he looked exhausted.

"I'm well. How's life with the new baby?" She had figured the infant might be the source for the bags under his eyes.

Fort reached into his shirt pocket and took out his phone. "Have you seen these pictures? She can't get any cuter." He stood next to Ellie and swiped through pages of photos. Lorelei Rose Besingame was a cherub-faced, rosy-cheeked, dark-haired bundle of happiness. It was hard to imagine the smiley baby anything but happy.

"She's always smiling," Ellie said.

"Until we try to go to sleep and then she is *not* happy. Fussiest thing ever. I actually took a nap in the jail cell yesterday. Don't tell Cori." He whispered the last part conspiratorially.

Grams waved at him. "Come show me those baby pictures and then tell us what brings you here."

Fort did as she requested. He took the rocking chair next to Grams, letting her scroll through his pictures. Ellie climbed the porch stairs, sat on the middle step, and turned sideways to face them.

"Remember that coyote Shane was helping us look for?" Fort said as he rocked slowly in the chair. He paused to yawn.

Fort continued, "Well, turns out we were right when he thought it might be a mountain lion. Lester Phillips caught it on his night camera. Went after one of his calves." He grimaced. "At least we can put those silly rabid coyote rumors to rest. Anyway, I thought I'd come by and warn ya. Might want to keep the goats locked up at night. He's been spotted at twilight a few times as well."

Ellie glanced at the yard and pasture. Her mare, Winnie, and their gelding, Puck, would not stay in the corral overnight until after this lion was caught. She'd keep them and Dolly the llama in the barn at night, no matter how many times Dolly kicked at her stall. Ellie's goats were running like banshees in the fenced yard. With the extra cash from the mineral lease, Ellie had a small room built off the laundry. Mudroom in design except the space was for goats and not dirty boots and coats. She wasn't taking any more chances with her little loves, or any of the animals for that matter. "Will do. Thanks, Fort."

He nodded. "We also have a new Game and Fish Warden. Started this week. You might see him around. He's made the mountain lion his priority."

"Finally," Grams said and slapped her knees. "Well, thanks for the heads up. I think I'll head over to Lester's and see if he needs anything." Grams shuffled into the house.

Fort and Ellie shared a smile.

"I saw them at the diner the other night when I was picking up some dinner." He raised a brow.

Ellie shook her head and laughed. "I think they're going steady. They sit out here on the porch, holding hands and laughing. It's great to see." Her heart ached from both happiness for Grams and heartache for herself.

"You hear from Shane?" Fort asked.

Ellie shook her head. "Its for the best, really." She continued when Fort shot her a questioning look. "Neither of us wants what the other does. For one of us to give up their dream would only create resentment. How long would anything last with resentment the foundation?"

"I can see your logic." He sighed wearily, then stood. "Much as

I'd like to sit here all day, maybe even take a nap, I gotta get back to the office." Fort stretched.

"Want some coffee or anything to go?" Ellie asked.

He shook his head. "See ya around." He slowly made his way to his truck.

Ellie laughed. Fort's misery was the happy kind, caused by a much-wanted change. She'd give anything to have that. Ellie refused to let herself get pulled into the doldrums, as Grams liked to call them. She reminded herself of all the good things she had in life. Funny how she was right where she wanted to be yet no longer had the same level of contentment. Ellie waved as Fort drove away then looked out at the foothills. Maybe, one day, she'd be fully happy again like she'd been before. Trouble was, it was hard once one knew what they were missing.

ONE WEEK LATER

E llie's schedule had lightened with the return of the Williams. She tried to fill the extra time with things she enjoyed. That was one thing Shane had been right about —she did work too much. She had one project left for the night before the sun set, to mend a fence board Winnie had kicked and broken, and then she'd reward herself with either a good book or movie.

Ellie gave a quiet "whoop," laughing at herself. Her night's fun was a book or a movie. Ellie was really living it up, but she conceded it was something. And it wasn't work. She wasn't ready for the dating scene. She hadn't been keen on it prior to Shane, and she definitely wasn't interested in it after him. She might, however, take the girls up on the book club they'd started. Soon, but not yet. She wasn't ready for all the company.

Though there was no news about the mountain lion, it had been a week since the attack at Phillips's farm and Ellie knew if the lion was a momma and there were cubs, another incident was pending unless the lion could bring down a pronghorn or a deer. Ellie could only hope.

She was leading Dolly toward the barn, the sun slowly slipping behind the Tetons, when she caught sight of movement across the meadow at the break of trees that led to the foothills.

Ellie paused, squinting. She was pretty confident it wasn't a mountain lion since their coats weren't red. The flash of red disappeared behind a patch of trees. Ellie waited to see if she could get another look. In one breath, the red object broke free from the trees and came into the meadow.

Ellie let out breath. It was a man on a horse. His light gray Stetson and red shirt and blue jeans looked familiar, and Ellie's mind clicked with the answer. This was the uniform of the Game and Fish Department. Looked like she was about to meet the new warden. Ellie continued her work and got Dolly settled into the barn, the horses already in their stalls. She checked the doors, closing the back one behind her as she stepped out. It was the best she could do to secure the animals at night. The goats were already in their pen inside the house. After donning work gloves, Ellie dragged the new fence board to the fence and worked on fitting it in the grooves of the post. She pushed on the center, trying to get it to bow slightly so it would pop into the groove to fit snugly. Then she'd nail gun the woven wire to the board. It was a delicate balance for a fence to be high enough with durability to keep Dolly and the goats in while not hurting wildlife, like deer, should they jump over. Ellie knew an electric fence was in the future. But for now this would do. The board finally popped in. Ellie smiled with satisfaction and lifted the woven wire. She aligned the nail and pulled the trigger, but nothing happened. The gun had jammed. She pounded the fence in frustration.

She paused as the sound of the horse drew closer. She glanced over her shoulder, then straightened, stretching to get a better look. Something about him, more than the uniform, was familiar. The broad stretch of his shoulders, the horse he was riding. Ellie wasn't expecting him so her mind was slow to put the pieces together. It wasn't until Shane was a handful of feet away and pulling back on Joe's reins that her brain finally computed what she was seeing.

"You trying to will the wire to nail itself?" Shane said with a lazy smile.

He looked good in the uniform. So good. She drank him in with her eyes, thinking there was a good chance this was all a dream.

"What are you doing here?" she asked.

He pointed to the tan, furry blanket stretched across the hindquarters of Joe. Only it wasn't a blanket. It was a mountain lion. "Sadly, I'm dealing with this guy. Looks like our night stalker was sick."

The lion's rib cage was prominent as was the pelvic girdle.

"Malnourished? How can that be with having just taken down a calf?" Ellie hated to see an animal down but reminded herself this was a harsh land and a rugged life. Peacefully coexisting with the wildlife was a balance that could be tipped by fire, drought, or illness. The root causes were endless. The unnecessary death of any animal was the last resort.

Shane shrugged and slid off Joe. "I'll let the guys in the lab figure that out. He was stalking a campground when I found him. Bunch of kids there playing."

Ellie gasped. She couldn't bring herself to imagine what might have happened. "Wait, you still haven't answered my question. Why are you *here*, here."

He stepped toward her, his lips quirking up to the side. "You mean why aren't I in California shooting guns with Marines?" He backed her up to the fence, narrowing the distance between them to two inches. He smiled down at her.

"Yeah," she said, breathy from the rapid beating of her heart. He looked good in his red chamois warden shirt. Brought out his dark eyes.

"Well, you see, there's this girl. Back home. I couldn't stop thinking about her." He tugged at one of the corkscrew ringlets that had broken free from her ponytail.

"Lucky girl," Ellie said. "I bet you're a hard one to forget, too."

Shane narrowed the space by an inch. "I sat at my commanding officer's desk and was presented with two options. One being active duty with an instructor position. As much as I fought that idea, it was a good job. It would've been better than I thought."

"What was the other option?" She couldn't take a deep breath. The air around her seemed thin, and she felt lightheaded with anticipation. Maybe even joy.

"To take a medical discharge." He closed the space, his hands coming to her hips, their chests pressed against each other.

She inhaled him, hoping to capture the feel and scent of him for when she woke up. No way, this wasn't a dream. "And you took the medical discharge?"

"That's where the girl comes in." He ducked slightly to kiss under her chin. "See," he said as he brushed kisses across her jawline, "I thought about how I could spend my days with stinky Marines shooting up stuff or my nights with a sexy farm girl. I picked the farm girl."

She wrapped her arms around his neck. Touching him felt good, felt right. Brought back that bit of light that had extinguished when he left. "What about the days?" she asked, still needing reassurance.

"I get to spend those with her, too. I get to be on the land I love, with the people I love." He looked her in the eyes.

"I bet your Mom, Dad, and Cricket are happy with your decision." She didn't want to think about the L word and how he might be applying it to her. She knew she felt love for him, try as she might to deny it.

"Yeah, they are. But that's not who I was talking about, cute-face." He tugged her closer, if that was possible. "I love you, Ellie Greene. It happened so fast I didn't believe it was true. But when I saw you banged up in your truck that day, I knew. I was too scared to admit it. Then when Landry pulled that gun on you, I lost all doubt. For the first time in my life my finger quivered on the trigger. I was scared I was going to screw up and lose you." He slanted his mouth over hers, kissing her with all he had.

Ellie couldn't get close enough to him. Couldn't get enough of his taste. When they broke free she rested her forehead on his shoulder. One niggling doubt remained. "But you left," she whispered.

"Yeah, because I was scared. I was scared that my injury and situation was affecting my feelings. I wasn't going to be less than you deserved. I was going to be all in or I was going to be a miserable bastard for the rest of my life. I took that medical discharge and haven't looked back. I'd have been here sooner but the government and all its bureaucratic red tape had me stuck in Cody for training the last few days." He stepped back and cupped her face in his hands.

"I'm all in cute-face. Every bit of me belongs to you. Carbon fiber parts and all."

She stretched up and kissed him softly on the lips, his hands sliding down her back. "I love you, Shane. Now take me home," she said, jumping up to wrap her legs around his waist.

EPILOGUE

ONE YEAR LATER

Ellie stood on the back deck, her hair twisted in a French knot, her makeup impeccably done. She clutched a bouquet of wildflowers bursting in colors of yellow, purple, blue, and white. She shifted nervously on her heels, wobbling slightly. She was fairly certain she was going to fall down the steps. She was a boots kinda girl. These heels, though small in height, were awkward.

Her tea-length dress, off white and made from chiffon with a V-neck, had a simple design, but not plain, like her. Shane stood in the yard, waiting for her. His Stetson was also off-white, his sports jacket a medium gray, his pants a shade darker. He'd chosen not wear his Marine uniform, since he was no longer active duty. Ellie didn't care if they said their vows in their birthday suits. She was desperate to make him hers. Not that the wedding mattered all that much. She didn't need a piece of paper to tell her she had to love him forever, because she would. She knew that beyond a shadow of a doubt. She also knew he felt the same way. This ceremony was more for their family and the children they would one day have.

Music began to play, and her dad extended his arm. Ellie looped hers through.

"You were right, Ell's," he said softly in her ear, "this is where you belong."

Having her father say it was nice, but she didn't need him to tell her something she already knew.

Ellie looked at Grams standing next to Lester Phillips. They'd tied the knot six months ago, and Grams had moved into Lester's place, making it their home, leaving the farm to Ellie and Shane. Grams smiled, then kissed her two fingers before touching her heart. She pointed those fingers at Ellie. Ellie did the same, tears springing forward. She knew she was blessed.

Ellie looked at Shane. He beamed and held out his hand. Ellie and her dad made their way to him. Her father lifted her hand from his arm and placed it in Shane's. She moved to stand close to him.

Shane leaned forward. "You're not thinking of running away are you?" He winked.

"Never," she said. "You're stuck with me forever." She leaned forward and kissed him.

"Stop!" Sabrina, who was officiating the ceremony, said with a laugh. "That part comes at the end."

The small crowd of their closest friends laughed. Shane's friend from the Marines, JT, was also there.

"Then get to it, will ya?" Shane said to Sabrina while taking Ellie's other hand so he held them both. He kissed her knuckles, looked Ellie in the eyes, and said, "Though loving you forever started the day I saw you with that flat tire."

ALSO BY KRISTI ROSE

The Wyoming Matchmaker Series

The Cowboy Takes A Bride

The Cowboy's Make Believe Bride

The No Strings Attached Series

The Girl He Knows

The Girl He Needs

The Girl He Wants

The Meryton Matchmakers Series

Meryton Matchmakers Book 1

Meryton Matchmakers Book 2

Meryton Matchmakers Book 3

Meryton Matchmakers Book 4

Honeymoon Postponed: A Mr. & Mrs. Darcy Adventure

Matchmaker's Guidebook - FREE

The Second Chance Short Stories can be read alone and go as follows:

Second Chances

Once Again

Reason to Stay

He's the One

Kiss Me Again

or purchased in a bundle for a better discount.

The Coming Home Series: A Collection of 5 Second Chance Short Stories

(Can be purchased individually).

Love Comes Home

ABOUT THE AUTHOR

Kristi Rose was raised in central Florida on boiled peanuts and iced tea. Kristi likes to write about the journeys of everyday people and the love that brings them together. Kristi is always looking for avid readers who are willing to do beta reads (give impression of story before edits) and advance readers who are willing to leave reviews. If you are interested, please sign up for her newsletter. Aside from her eternal gratitude she also likes to do giveaways as well.

You can connect with Kristi at any of the following:
www.kristirose.net
kristi@kristirose.net

JOIN MY NEWSLETTER

AND GET A FREE BOOK

Hi

If you'd like to be the first to know about my sales and new releases then join my newsletter. As part of my reader community you will have access to giveaways, freebies, and bonus content.

Sound like you might be interested? Give me a try. You can always unsubscribe at any time.

www.kristirose.net

XOXO,

Kristi

CARE TO LEAVE A REVIEW?

Dear Reader,

I am so honored that you took the time to read my book. If you feel so inclined, I would appreciate it if you left an honest review. You don't have to say much. Put the stars you feel it deserves and a few words. Some folks don't even put words. Reviews go a long way in helping authors in all sorts of areas including marketing.

Thanks again. You're a rock star!

Have a great one.

Kristi

Made in the USA
Middletown, DE
12 April 2020

88951230R00128